THE INLARI SAGAS

ARMISTICE

M. J. KELLEY
DANA LEIPOLD

ELAINE CHAO
WOELF DIETRICH

kōsa press

Published by
Kōsa Press
www.kosapress.com
Kosa Media, LLC
San Francisco, CA, USA, & Hastings, Hawke's Bay, New Zealand

For more information, please contact the publisher at info@kosapress.com.

Edited by Ally Bishop
Cover design by Arthur Haas
Book layout by Creative Kook Designs

ISBN: 978-0-9941240-1-2

First Edition: January 2017
10 9 8 7 6 5 4 3 2 1

CONTENTS

TIMELINE

BFC – BEFORE FIRST CONTACT ON EARTH
AFC – AFTER FIRST CONTACT ON EARTH

2 MILLION YEARS BFC
Inlarah, last known original inlari world, destroyed by the Rordorah.

1.75 MILLION YEARS BFC
Landing on Lenti, first post-Inlarah planet. Rordorah destroys it.

975 THOUSAND YEARS BFC
Landing on Nep, the sixth post-Inlarah planet. Rordorah destroys it.

750 THOUSAND YEARS BFC
The Great Split: the fleet separates.

600 THOUSAND YEARS BFC
First contact with the hostile species boleeron on Feralu.

121 YEARS BFC
Again, the boleeron attack Naru, the eighth post-Inlarah planet.

2 YEARS BFC
Space-time warping technology is achieved for the first time.

0 YEAR

First contact: the inlaris arrive on Earth.

1 YEAR AFC

Inlaris strike a pact with the nations of Earth to trade technology for refuge.

3 YEARS AFC

The human-inlari built *Veggo* launches to retrieve the rest of the fleet.

20 YEARS AFC

Some of the nations of Earth request that the inlaris distribute technology fairly or leave.

43 YEARS AFC

Inlaris accepted into Australia and New Zealand and most migrate there.

50-58 YEARS AFC

The Great Earth/Inlari War.

58 YEARS AFC

Weapons of mass destruction ravage most of Earth's surface. Starships and warp technology are lost, as well as other technologies.

61 YEARS AFC

Inlari extremists take over in New Zealand and make arrangements to enslave the human population.

62 YEARS AFC

Naven expels all inlaris from its walls and isolates itself from the world.

63 YEARS AFC

Thaddeus James' revolution begins in Queensland.

108 Years AFC

When *Interspecies* takes place.

157 Years AFC

When "The Carrion Hunter" takes place.

INTRODUCTION

Long before humans walked the earth, an interstellar civilization curled its roots through a small patch of the galaxy. The inlaris flourished. Proud, relentless, ruthless, they explored the stars, conquering whatever sentient beings lay in their path. But as planets turn to dust and stars shrink or burst, so too did the inlari empire pass on. The undoing was gradual, spontaneous, limbs of a body going to sleep, and then quietly falling away, never to be roused again.

Only the homeworld remained—Inlarah. And for a time, peace thrived. Contentment and well-being reigned. But it didn't last. Catastrophe soon sent the inlaris back into the deep of space, this time not to conquer and spread, but to fight, escape, and survive. Relentlessly pursued, extinction forever looming, they struggled for a solution. If they could not beat their foe, they would outrun it.

With the advent of space-time warping, the inlaris felt salvation was near. The technology heralded a new era of peace, a time to cease fighting—an age of armistice. Their test ships jumped from promising system to promising system, searching for habitable planets. And then they stumbled upon a small world in an obscure part of the galaxy—a world we know as Earth.

EXODUS

M.J. KELLEY

63 YEARS AFC

"MOLO," THE LITTLE ones chant. "Come out." Children, horns barely budding, splash about my abode, kicking the flimsy plastic walls, staining my haunt's perimeter with muddy toe prints.

Rain.

My ceiling canopy leaks rain. The gradual drops transform the powdery dirt floor to mud. Outside, the dirt streets flow with water instead of feet, arbitrarily forging new tributaries through the reservation, spreading runnels between the yellow-pink habitats.

Collected haphazardly, only inches between their plastic walls, the habitats canvas the treeless land like the curved shells of earthen, half-submerged clams.

"Molo," they shout. The children's name for me. Means old one.

"Stop kicking my walls."

The runts enter without invitation, asking, "Are you really as old as they say?" Asking, "Are you truly from the homeworld?"

One brings me a water-filled saucepan. I raise my head. I drink, the cool liquid assuaging my irritation. What are their names? Over time, too many to remember.

What can I tell them?

"The last known homeworld." I sit up in my cot. "I'm the oldest still living. I'm older than Yedrik, who is one hundred and one Earth years. Yet, I'm only ninety-four myself." The children laugh, the impossibility tickling their minds.

I tell them that I lived in blinks and slept frozen in the emptiness between stars. Nine times the new ones woke me from my frozen tomb. Nine foreign stars I saw rise above the surfaces of worlds now lost. Ninety-four Earth years, I tell them. But I've lived for millions more. Twice, I've died.

I point at a girl. "Your age? About eight? I was eight when the stars went black, when the gas giant Glypto disappeared as if the vacuum of space had washed away its great hydrogen storms, banishing the planet from sight."

I tell them at age ten, I woke to our world—tiny Inlarah—in death throes, black rocks crackling across the sky, igniting our atmosphere, a fire shower hiding our sun.

Imagine a long silver dome reflecting the sky's turmoil, its curved ceiling arching for many miles, thousands of shuttles inside waiting to evacuate you to the stars. The reflective dome looked as if it were only the top of a great sphere, the rest buried below ground. Queues of millions streamed toward its curved ceiling, like fingered rivers draining in from multiple lakes. Vessels with amaranthine glows fired out of the spaceport, blasting their engines, rocketing underneath the bombardment of black rock and fire.

From space, Inlarah's purple-crimson beauty bled out against the darkness, its oceans evaporating into white vapor. And then Inlarah was gone. Cut from existence. Swallowed by the Rordorah.

My mother pulled me from the starship's window, pressing my face to her abdomen. She did not want me to see, but she was too late. Some people dropped to their knees. An elderly male dug his horns into the ship's deck, scraping back and forth in anguish as cries and shouts rose and fell all around.

My parents put me into one of the few remaining cryotubes. I awoke, still a child, hundreds of thousands of years later—everyone I once knew, dead. You see, that is why I'm so old.

I tell the children that generations spawned, lived, and died on the starships; the *Memoriams* recorded and passed on the knowledge of our exodus as we escaped to an unexplored system. They froze us, froze me, to save our culture, to preserve something physical of who we were. The new generations trained the old, trained us to fight, to survive—the whole time, the new star peeked through our ship's windows, growing brighter.

We lasted one year on Lenti's dry plains before the stars, again, disappeared. The Rordorah pursued us. Hoping to slow its edging mass, we flung continent-sized asteroids into its dark immensity, but the rocks were swallowed, like Inlarah. We escaped again, our fleet plunging back into the emptiness. Again I climbed into my tube, hoping to never see the Rordorah return. But the stars vanished on five more worlds before we split our fleet. Three groups, three different stars. We hoped the Rordorah couldn't follow us all.

The seventh time, I awoke on Feralu's flat ice drifts. We survived two years, but the boleeron came. A wholly different menace from the Rordorah. A violent, vicious race, one the zealots thought the Rordorah had spawned—I fought them too, and lost, my ship flayed by their weapons, diced and stripped away around me, my body flung from the splintering pieces. I tumbled into space. My people found me adrift. I died for the first time, my mind preserved, my life resurrected later.

The tenth time, I awoke to Trenar's immense clouds and oceans, its green and yellow continents. Trenar, the world humans call Earth. "Your tube is no longer needed," the new ones told me. Our ships, our technology, my cryotube—the new ones traded to the humans for sanctuary. They released me from my eternal sleep, freed me from my duty to defend. Did they know my true age? What I had seen?

We watched the stars, but the threat came from the surface. It was not the boleeron, nor the Rordorah that decimated Earth. It was war.

My cot creaks as I recline against the wet plastic. Freed from the storyteller's trance, I find myself alone, my abode dark. When did the children leave? Over the years, the little ones' faces change, but their curiosity is the same. They patter in and ask and ask.

What shall I tell them? What must they know?

The rain abandons us. Powdery dirt coats my floor again. I drape myself in bedding and part the door flaps. The stars spread in a thick band along the sky's apex. "We are pursued no more," the new ones told me years ago.

But right there, an immense blackness, like a hole, overlays part of the starry sky.

My heart lurches.

"Where are the stars?" I want to shake the other habitats, wake the reservation. "Is no one watching? Rordorah's found us!" I try to remember the route to the spaceport, try to see its silver arc beyond the round-roofed habitats. But the reservation is quiet, dark. Everyone sleeps. The night is windless. The black spot vanishes, and the stars return. More black spots, much smaller, slip across the stars. There is no Rordorah, only clouds passing on a high wind, only memories grasping at my throat, only my ancient blood shouting: run. But this is Earth.

There'll be no running now.

WHEN STARS BLINK

WOELF DIETRICH

0 YEAR

THEY ARRIVED IN two spaceships. Larger than New York City, each carried over five million alien beings. One crash-landed in Los Angeles and destroyed the city.

The other came down in the Tonto National Park in Arizona, leaving a monstrous furrow rivaling the Grand Canyon in its wake.

They came out of nowhere. No contact, no message or warning. Just appeared between our moon and us one night. I lay stargazing on my roof, as I used to do on those sticky, summer nights, gazing up at the clear night sky dusted with shimmering stars. I remember how full and bright the moon shone: pale blue light illuminated the landscape, causing even the hardiest of shadows to shrink behind bushes and scrubs and knee-high boulders.

A thunderous crack shattered the calm, airless night. The sky folded in on itself, and those millions of scattered stars disappeared, leaving an emptiness so ominous it seemed alive.

Suddenly, as though giving birth, the void cracked wide, and those two behemoths spilled out.

I glimpsed something behind them in that moment before the portal closed. A gaping maw, dark red like dried blood, loomed behind those ships, but disappeared just as quickly. The stars flickered back to life, and the night was clear and bright once more.

You'd think with all the science fiction movies and art, we'd have an inkling of what to expect. But nothing prepared me for the spectacle I witnessed. As the spaceships entered our space and burst through the ozone layer, looking more like flying whales than spaceships, a screeching howl pierced the night air and roared through the valleys and hills, tearing the windows out of their panes. The roof shuddered under me, spilling my beer where I had left it untouched next to me.

We would later learn they call themselves inlari, which means "Children of the Great Star." We also discovered they had warped from a neighboring galaxy and miscalculated the jump, almost colliding with Earth. It would have been devastating to both species had they exited the warp-jump in our atmosphere.

The Earth came very close to annihilation that day, but most people would never know. All they saw were alien spaceships crash-landing on Earth. There was excitement, mass hysteria, fear, jubilations, suicides, religious debates, and a revolution or two. New religions sprang up overnight, and others became irrelevant.

What did it matter, though? Our world would be destroyed fifty years later. Now, as an arthritic old man, immobile with age and old wounds, when I think of all that has transpired since, all the blood that has spilled, that has soaked deep into our collective memory as a species, I wish we had died that night when the stars blinked.

HEELS ON FIRE

DANA LEIPOLD

51 YEARS AFC

HE NESTLED NEXT to his mother as she read him his favorite story, the one about the hero, Kantos, and his adventures on Naru. She embraced him. Her smell, a mixture of citrus and mint, made him feel safe, like a warm blanket on a crisp evening.

Then he was hurled into the air by a powerful force and deafening sound. Glass, concrete, and debris rained down on him as his body slammed into the ground, and he struggled to catch his breath. The ringing in his ears and pain in his chest made it difficult to orient himself. He tasted metallic ooze and curled into a ball.

Figures tromped through the haze and eerie silence, approaching him like ominous clouds. Fighting through the pain, he limped away, flashing glances over his shoulder. The crunching of heavy boots on rubble continued as he stumbled over blown-out bits of rubble from his home. He tripped, falling face-first into a pile of burned fabric, inhaling the ashes and choking until he nearly vomited. It was the robe his mother had been wearing just a few moments ago.

He felt someone grab his shirt and lift him upright. Tears streamed down his face, and he couldn't focus his vision as he gasped for air.

"Mother?" He called in Anshahar.

The figure had no horns. Large, ominous eyes peered at him like he was an animal. He remembered mother's warnings about humans. She told him to never trust them, and if he ever ran into one, he should run like his heels were on fire. He tried to squirm his way out of the human's grasp, but he was no match for this one's strength.

"It's just a child. Let's take it back to base and let them figure out what to do with it."

"Just kill it."

"No, that would be against orders."

He understood what the human said into the communication device, and breathed a sigh of relief.

The human dragged him toward a group standing like vultures next to a large vehicle.

"Did you find any more?"

"Just one."

Unlatching the door to the vehicle, the human threw him into the dark cabin. He plowed into the wall as the doors closed. After a moment, he sensed he was not alone. Though he could not see, he opened his arms reaching toward the sound of sobbing.

"Mother!"

"Rojai!"

Rojai felt his way into an urgent embrace, some of the shock washing away as he melted into her arms.

"My child! Thank the Great Star—you're alive!"

"Are we going to die?"

The vehicle lurched forward, and they toppled over. Cold, hard metal crashed into the side of his face. Then his mother helped him sit up, and he felt her hand on his cheek.

"They attacked us. I don't know where they are taking us. But I won't let anything bad happen to you." She sucked in her breath. "No matter what happens, my sweet Rojai, you run like your heels are on fire when I tell you to, okay?"

"But what about you? What are you going to do?"

"I'll be right behind you. Just keep running. I'll follow."

Her arms enveloped him, and, for a moment, he felt safe in the darkness. They bumped and jerked around on the harsh metal bed. To Rojai, it seemed as if they had been traveling for an eternity. When the vehicle came to a stop, they heard voices and footsteps, then the latch. Rojai's heart pounded. Blinding light flooded the space, and he couldn't see the arms that grabbed him, pulling him from the vehicle.

Blinking, he struggled and called out for his mother. He spotted her next to him. She kicked and screamed against the two humans holding her, and somehow, she broke free, lunging like a rabid animal at the human who had him by the arm. She wrestled his captor to the ground, turned her head and yelled in Anshahar.

"Run Rojai! Now! I will follow!"

Without thinking, he sprinted as if he were escaping the clutches of a blazing inferno. Fueled by a terror he couldn't understand, he fled toward the hills without looking back. He ran like Kantos, with god-like speed until he heard the shots echo. He halted in his tracks, then whipped around to see his mother's body, still and crumpled on the ground. The humans spotted him.

He ran despite his panic and tears. He ran for his life, not knowing where he was going. He would never stop running. Even as his feet were ripped apart by the rocks and harsh earth, he knew he would never stop.

THE ENVOYS

M.J. KELLEY

3 YEARS AFC

T HE STARSHIP Veggo looked like an ancient modernist hotel
when seen from certain angles, windows randomly arranged
on the sides and uneven humps rising above the hull. The ship's
length was ten city blocks and its height thirty stories in some
places.

Tim's neck ached from gazing up at the ship's gray-purple
surface. The sun's morning light reflected on the craft's skin as
they drove toward it in the two-seater rover.

They drove beneath an overhang and into shadow, the overhang
reminding Tim of a stingray's great flap. Inlari and human crews
bustled around the ship's landing frame, performing tests and
last-minute retrofits. Seeing the ship up close, Tim still couldn't
fathom his luck at being selected for this mission.

ONLY THREE YEARS AGO, ELIZA WATCHED THE SMOKE RISE ABOVE

Los Angeles like a black storm. Military helicopters and jets took over the sky, investigating the destruction. An attack? A meteor? Neither.

She was a linguist, a tenure-track professor when she joined the first contact team. The two inlari ships were damaged beyond repair, but many hundreds of thousands of inlaris had survived the crashes. In the early days of their meetings, the horned aliens spoke to Eliza about how their space-time jump technology was new. They'd been testing it, hoping it would save their species from additional eons of interstellar survival.

Now Eliza stood next to Tim on the platform, posing for hundreds of cameras. They wore metallic-like space suits resembling futuristic bodies of armor, helmets tucked under their arms. The wind ruffled the flags of the world behind them as they smiled. In front of them, thousands of humans and aliens assembled on the great landing pad. Spectators had come to witness this induction and see Earth's first ever inter-species mission team. Veggo, the culmination of inlari ingenuity and vast human resources, rested mightily to their left. The inlari executive team accompanied Eliza and Tim. Although the ship was Earth funded and built, its technology belonged to the inlari, and so the newly arrived aliens would be commanding the mission.

Human members of the International Veggo Mission Committee gave speeches at a thin, glass lectern. "It has taken an unprecedented world effort..." "A galactic partnership forged in team work..." "A truly historic undertaking, the likes of which Earth has never seen."

In the short years since Eliza had encountered these creatures, she worked with them as they lobbied nations, seeking funds and resources to build a new ship for a singular mission: bring the rest of the fleet back. The nations of Earth, led by the United States, agreed in exchange for technology and alien knowledge, hoping both would soothe the ailing world economy.

THE VEGGO LAUNCHED FROM FLORIDA ON A CLOUDLESS DAY, BLUE-white smoke trailing behind as both humans and inlaris watched from Earth's surface. Inside, Eliza and Tim reclined in launch chairs as the starship rattled around them. Once space enveloped the Veggo—Earth but a receding speck—the mission leader invited them to dine with the inlari executive crew.

They entered the lab that had been transformed into an eating hall. The inlaris held drinking flutes, long, skinny glasses containing *shiad,* a drink that caused hallucinations in humans.

The inlaris were draped in loose, semitransparent tunics of lightly colored, flowing materials. Tim and Eliza, in their stiff, elegant suits, stopped and looked around, smiling awkwardly. Then a crooning wavered from the inlaris' mouths and echoed in the hall like some sing-song melody. They took short breaks from this performance to drink from flutes, their heads nodding up and down as if in a hypnotic trance.

"I think we're overdressed," Eliza whispered as they glanced around for guidance.

As suddenly as this vocal symphony had come, it ceased. Three inlari broke from the group and took the arms of Eliza and Tim, escorting them to their seats around a large table. The table curved intricately through the rest of the lab like a river, its surface carved with spiraling rivets.

Eliza and Tim each sat next to an inlari translator.

"What was that...sound? At the start?" Tim asked Itha, his appointed translator.

"We were welcoming you." Four horns extended from the back of Itha's skull, two at the top like a regular inlari, but then an additional set that curved downward and then forward, reflecting the top set.

The meal was served in silence, and between courses, a brown powder in wide, flat saucers was presented in front of each attendee. The inlaris rubbed the powder on their horns and pushed it into their nostrils. They then dabbed their necks with water.

Eliza and Tim followed suit as best they could. The brown powder stung Tim's skin and caused a rash that he then dabbed with water. Eliza's eyes watered, long tears streaming down, brown smudges on the rims of her nostrils.

Tim reached for his flute and drank deeply. The water tasted sour and had a creamy texture. When he gazed up from the flute, he noticed that everyone had stopped eating. They stared at him.

"That was my flute," said Itha. "And it was filled with *shiad*."

The table erupted with gleeful howls.

Reaching for a long vine hanging above the table, Itha twisted a spigot on the end, and then filled Tim's flute with more *shiad*. "Now there's no excuse. Drink up. Have the full experience."

Next, *wartella* seeds, as big as human hands; *catum,* a meaty, cotton candy-like thing; *arrumo,* drunk from a spigot; *asolo* noodle trees; *flamango,* a hearty plant once grown on Inlarah; *facali,* a cheesy cream vegetable encrusted with shingle-like fat.

Toward the end of the meal, Tim found it difficult to concentrate and asked to be excused. Itha walked him to his room, where he spent the night with stomach cramps and strange visions.

After weeks of testing in space, the Veggo was ready.

Eliza and Tim climbed into red suits made from a spongy material. Once inside, their helmets descended and locked around their neck rings, an oxygen mask slipped over their faces, and then the suits filled with a creamy liquid that foamed around their bodies.

"I always feel like a marshmallow person," Eliza said over their comm.

"Or a sumo wrestler?" Tim chuckled.

They'd trained in these radiation suits for months, but there was renewed excitement as this time it was for real—the first humans ever to experience a space-time jump, and the first to accompany an alien species into space.

Their suits lofted and became suspended between the ceiling and floor. Red lights dimmed in the circular command room, as many other suits lifted into suspension around them. Eliza imagined hanging in the pod-like suits was like being a seed inside a pomegranate. The suits glowed with a faint crimson light, very faint. She thought she could see the silhouetted bodies of the inlaris inside.

Beyond the suits was a circular window looking out upon the mass of stars. Moments later, those stars and the vast emptiness around them curved into a sphere. The sphere's edges lit with gravitational lensing, bending the stars' incandescence into concentric, distorted rings, akin to seeing lights distorted through a water glass. Space collapsed forward, trailing diamond streams and catching Eliza mid-exhale. She couldn't close her mouth as time slowed outside her mind. Tim started to say something, but his voice rang in one continuous note as the sphere swallowed the Veggo in a sudden, accelerated flash.

Red, blue, green lights swept the command hall, enveloping the dangling radiation suits in swaths of strobing color. Eliza felt as if a bubble popped in her mind, as if the dimension she knew existed only within her own perception, the constructs of which she had momentarily escaped.

A new blanket of stars shimmered outside the window as though they'd always been there.

"Here we go." Tim's words finally completed their sounds.

Eliza finished her exhale, closing her mouth as her time perception returned to normal.

PARTLY OBSCURED BEHIND HYDROGEN CLOUDS, SHAPES OF ROUND, porpoise-like vessels, large flat carriers, and oblong cruisers drifted together like precious stones flung across black velvet. The entirety of the inlari fleet adrift. Some vessels were all engine, their giant cylinders offering little comfort for a small crew. Others were square, and still others boasted translucent, angelic hulls, winged serpents, brightly colored exotic fish.

ONE BY ONE, THE SHIPS WERE DISMANTLED IN SPACE, AND NEW galactic components were produced with 3D printers the size of small towns. Inlari teams disassembled the huge rings around one engine and held them suspended in space as another team slowly moved the enormous components and new warp apparatus into the opening.

While inlari crews updated the fleet, Tim and Eliza visited the various vessels, giving translated talks and distributing Earth educational materials. They spoke with the fleet's leadership council, and Tim gave an impassioned speech on how the two species could learn from one another. They accompanied Itha, too, as she visited the other ships. Eliza and Itha invented an English word for Itha's other role—*Memoriam*. The *Memoriam* Order recorded and retained the history of the inlari species solely with their minds. Tim asked the *Memoriams* many questions, but found them secretive about their abilities, which he guessed were similar to having an eidetic memory.

SOON THE ENTIRE FLEET HAD BEEN RETROFITTED, AND THE MISSION leader invited Eliza and Tim to a private meeting. Two translators, including Itha, joined them.

"It is time for the fleet to visit Earth," the translator spoke for the mission leader. "But the Veggo will continue on."

"What does he—I mean, what do you mean by that?" Tim asked.

"Eons ago our fleet split into three to evade an ancient enemy, a pursuer. The other two fleets may still be out there. The Veggo's new mission will be to find them, retrofit their ships, and return to Earth." He paused and leaned forward. "The human species has shown us more kindness than we ever thought possible in this universe. The understanding we came to, for our technology to be exchanged for refuge, is precious to us. We will never forget it. As my people acclimate to Earth, humans will need to acclimate to us. Tell your people what you saw and experienced here. Tell them what our two species could be capable of if we work together."

AGAIN, ELIZA AND TIM FLOATED, COCOONED IN THE RED SUITS.

Space collapsed, sending stars into rings around a sphere as time slowed. Then Earth, in all its blue and cloud-swirled glory, floated before them. Despite their home planet's familiarity, they both felt a shift in how they viewed it. The world seemed simultaneously smaller and more preciously important than ever before. They would spend the rest of their lives striving to understand this feeling and what it meant for the world.

THE KORU

WOELF DIETRICH

63 YEARS AFC

I N THOSE FIRST years after the Great Inlari War, when displacement of peoples was necessary, when New Zealanders faced purging or enslavement, when their sovereignty dissolved overnight as if by some fickle afterthought; in those days, tears and sorrow saturated the land. Fire and ash brought scars no memory could ever wipe. New Zealanders naturally revolted as any people would when faced with theft of their homeland, their strength bolstered by Māori's warrior spirit.

They battled with weapons ancient and new, with a desperation bordering on the supernatural, and, for a short period, the two islands fell into a darkness of violence and despair as revolution tore at its heart, threatening to rip the country apart at the seams. Inlaris against humans. Humans against inlaris. Blood soaked the green valleys and black stygian shores, and Aotearoa bled into the ocean...

EDFA AND HER UNBORN CHILD STRUGGLED THROUGH THE DENSELY covered forest as labor pains tore at her abdomen. Sweat marred her face, and the thin gown plastered to her body impeded her movement as she navigated jutting roots and thorn-like underbrush. She could hear her pursuers thrashing behind her, shouting to one another, getting closer. She cradled her abdomen as branches whipped and tore at her. Her baby would be the first of her family born here on Earth.

Desperation spurred her on. They were close now. Cracking branches and human voices echoed behind her.

"She's nearby!"

To her left, a small hill veined by tree roots and covered by a thick layer of bright green moss offered hope. She scrambled up, using protruding roots for purchase and clawing through the moss, digging her fingers into the wet soil underneath, slipping as another stab of pain wracked her body. She almost lost her footing, and a deep groan erupted from her lips.

"I heard something! This way!"

Fear drove her forward, and she crawled in a frenzied rush over the top. Too late she realized the other side disappeared into a deep ravine. She tumbled down the dark gorge, hitting tree trunks and ferns and thick roots, until a cracking pain against her head took her sight and sound, and even the pain of labor could not keep her from losing consciousness.

Convulsions brought Edfa back to life with a start. Pain tunneled through her body, forcing her to stifle a scream, turning it into a low moan that crawled up her windpipe and released into a pain-laced lament.

Soon. Her child's time is soon.

Edfa lay back, resting her head against the moss-covered trunk of an uprooted tree. The musky redolence of mold and damp earth filled her nostrils. A break in the forest canopy revealed a night sky shimmering with far-off galaxies and a full moon whose light shards danced brilliantly against the foliage surrounding her. She found herself in a clearing among a forest of Nothofagus trees and colossal ferns. Edfa no longer heard human voices, not even a faint whisper. She shuddered and bit her lip, clawing at the soggy leaf mold as another sharp cramp pealed through her worn body.

And then her water broke. *Her child was coming.*

Tears burst from her eyes and streaked her cheeks as a great sob of sorrow shook her lithe frame. Grief and fear. Her life partner, her parents—murdered by humans, and now, here on the soggy, leafy floor of an alien forest, she was about to give birth to the next generation of inlaris. She'd never felt this alone or so much fear. Her body spasmed as yet another wave of agony washed over her. This time, she could not contain the scream. Her song of childbirth echoed through the dense forest and reverberated down the gorges and creeks and valleys beyond.

"Oh Great Star! What am I to do?!" Fresh tears welled up in Edfa's eyes, and then another bolt of pain arched her back as her body tried to escape the pain of childbirth.

She could no longer see the night sky above her. A warm breeze pushed through the treetops, swaying them into a whispering dance that made the stars flicker and the moon's silver beams falter. The woods moved in towards her as their dance became erratic, and the wind more violent. Edfa tried to push back, but she was weak, and the pain in her belly had taken the life from her legs. She could do nothing. The baby was coming.

The winds subsided, and the trees stopped dancing, and the giant ferns became still once more, and Edfa was no longer alone. Startled by the appearance of a human next to her, Edfa shrank back. "Please, don't hurt me," she pleaded softly, her voice drained.

A human girl no older than twelve seasons knelt next to her. The girl's olive-skin was flawless like smooth velvet, and her long obsidian hair shimmered in the moon's half-light. She wore a waist girdle of animal skin and a lax cloak with vertical weft rows and little else. The pendant around her neck glowed a soft green. It was made of jade stone and carved into a swirl.

The girl studied her with eyes like molten gold, and kindness radiated from them like rays of sun after a stormy night.

The girl smiled. "You have nothing to fear, child—Rehua has sent me. Anahera will care for you now."

Edfa wanted to say something, but her words floundered as Anahera bent forward and stroked her forehead, her touch both cool and tender and something else. A comforting warmness flowed through Edfa's body, pushing the stabbing pain in her abdomen back further and further until it was nothing more than a dull pressure against her insides.

Anahera began chanting, her voice soft and soothing, uttering strange words that made no sense to Edfa, yet the girl's voice embraced her like a soft caress and spoke to the life inside of her. Fear and all the angst of the night untangled itself and withdrew from her, and she let go willingly. She lay back down, resting against the moss cushion of the rotting tree as Anahera's words echoed in her mind.

"Ka hinga atu he tete-kura—ka hara-mai he tete-kura."

It didn't matter that she didn't understand the words, for Anahera's voice gave assurance, made her feel safe and protected.

She felt her child move within her, but no panic formed or threatened to derail her thoughts. Just the dull ache pushing against the warm glow in her body.

The chanting continued, and after a while Efda realized the words no longer held any mystery:

As one fern frond dies—one is born to take its place.

The girl continued, and the throbbing kept pushing against the heat inside of her until at last Efda heard her baby's first squeak, then a loud wail as it entered the world, sounding both foreign and natural in the thick forest of tangled roots and shrubs.

Efda burst out crying as the girl placed her baby boy into her waiting arms. Tears of joy flowed then, streaking her cheeks and splashing onto her child's blood-smeared head, the faint buds visible proof of what would soon grow into beautiful inlari horns.

"Thank you!" Efda cried. "You've saved my son." The words spilled out, fueled by joy and relief.

Anahera smiled warmly. "You should thank Rehua. He interceded on your behalf." She stroked Efda's matted hair softly and pushed strands back from her wet face. She took the jade pendant from around her neck and slipped it over Edfa's head, resting it between her breasts. Anahera then stood, unclipped her cloak, and wrapped baby and mother tightly with it. "You will be safe here until your people find you tomorrow. You will not be discovered by your enemies."

"I'm so confused. You're not inlari, yet you speak Anshahar. Who are you?" Edfa stammered.

Anahera studied Edfa for a moment, her warm gaze soothing the inlari female. "I do not speak Anshahar, child, but Te Reo Māori, the language of my people."

"But how is it possible we understand each other?" Edfa's brain scrambled for logic, trying to make sense of the situation, of this human who exuded such warmth and radiance.

Anahera shrugged. "There are no language barriers in the spirit world, no words to hide behind. Rehua felt the anguish in your heart. He heard your unborn son's cries."

Before Edfa could ask, Anahera continued. "To Māori, Rehua is a star god. He who lives in the highest of the heavens. Some call him Antares or Sirius. You know him as the Great Star Inlar, the Life Giver. Rehua has many forms." Her words echoed in Edfa's mind from no direction and every direction.

Fresh tears rimmed her eyes. "Oh, Great Inlar! My family has been murdered by the humans just this night. I have only my child now, and he has no father. He has nothing." Her voice croaked with grief. "What will I do? What is to become of my son?"

Anahera's golden eyes dimmed for a moment and then brightened as she began to speak. "As one fern frond dies—one is born to take its place. Like the unfurling frond of a silver fern, Koru represents new life. The future and the past. It represents hope. You have everything, Edfa. In your arms, you hold a nation. But for now, you must sleep, for with sleep comes healing. Goodbye, Edfa. Rest well."

Edfa's limbs felt like heavy stones and she battled to keep her eyelids open. "Please, wait Anah..." but her voice trailed off as the figure of Anahera vanished, taken by a soft wind that made the trees dance once more. Sleep took Edfa while her son suckled her swollen breast.

The next morning, Edfa woke to her son's cries and a forest teeming with the noise of life. Lances of gold pierced the foliage, bathing her in a warm, soothing light. Positioning her nipple so her son could feed, Edfa listened to the symphony of sounds—from birdsong and weta rasps to the slow trickle of a brook nearby.

The previous night's violence seemed a world away. Her skin felt tight from dried sweat and blood which cracked when she moved. She looked down at her feeding child to adjust the cloak around him, but saw only her torn garment. She'd used her gown to cover her newborn baby boy. Her fingers touched her throat cautiously, but there was nothing. No jade pendant.

Edfa closed her eyes as she tried to recall what to her felt like a dream now, but found she had no clear memory. Everything felt hazy and out of focus. The only thing she knew with any certainty is that her son's name would be Koru.

FIRST STEPS

ELAINE CHAO

5 YEARS AFC

FOR THE FIRST time in hours, Mother was silent. She scanned the small shipboard apartment she had grown up in, a home she had kept after her parents died and Ghera was born. Others left in the days and weeks before, and finally, it was their turn to start their new lives planetside. Mother had packed two crates, one for herself and the other for Ghera, full of clothing and small keepsakes to remind them of their inlari heritage.

Ghera stared at the living room to fix it in her memory, bidding farewell to the stuffed *khima* toy that had been hers since she was a baby. There was no room for such things, and she was nearly grown now. Ghera blinked hard, but no matter how much she tried to subdue it, nervous anticipation beat under her breastbone like a little *inshali*, its four delicate wings fluttering in a rippling motion.

She and Mother joined Kannol, Ghera's uncle, in the corridor, and Ghera could barely contain her excitement. They were finally going to see Trenar—a real planet!—and the people there were called "humans." Apparently, they had their own name for the planet: "Earth."

Kannol worked in communications and knew all sorts of things about these humans. A couple of them had come on board as ambassadors, and Kannol had taken regular lessons in "English," one of the many strange tongues these aliens spoke. So many languages, and so many variations of them! Of course, Anshahar had many dialects, but at least all inlaris could understand each other.

He also said humans told time differently. She counted her age as ten solars, for example, but Trenar's—or Earth's, as he was quick to correct her—circuit around its sun was longer. She was only eight "years" old by their measure. It didn't make much difference to her: she had been born on this ship during a time when almost the entire inlari fleet had been stranded in the Deep.

Finally, she would get to see a planet. Everyone around her— well, the older ones, at least—had vague recollections of their last home, of Naru, but Ghera had no such memories. What was it like to breathe air that wasn't recycled? What was it like to see light that came from a star and not from a lamp? She asked Mother these questions all the time, but Mother had no answers.

Ghera and Mother stood in line with Kannol until they descended a long ramp. She could tell they were outside immediately: warm and laden with humidity, the air coated her skin and hair. She stepped from the ramp onto the ground, aware that she felt heavier than usual. This, Kannol had told her, was normal. Gravity on Trenar was different, and her body would need time to adjust. He also said humans could see a different type of color, as their eyes were adjusted for their yellow sun; Ghera noticed that the light was dimmer somehow, darker and brighter all at the same time. Knowing something and experiencing it were two different things, though. Ghera stood a little closer to Mother.

Then they were on a vessel that floated in the water like a toy, and Ghera clung to her mother's arm as the ferry glided past a tall green statue with the strangest horn pattern she'd ever seen. Humans must have horns, too! That made her feel a little better. Her stomach churned as the ferry hummed over the water, careening from side to side unpredictably. Why did everything move so strangely here?

Once the vessel docked, they crossed another ramp, and then they were in a city. The number of people! The lights! The noises! The smells! They passed her, faster and faster, until she felt faint. The smell of something foul mixed with something savory, and people—many different colors and shapes and sizes, none of them with horns and none of them stopping to greet the inlaris— charged to and fro in a cacophony of chatter. Buildings loomed so high that she couldn't even see the tops, crowding together like the huge towers of crates she used to wander through in the ship's hold. Enormous displays fought for her attention, blinking from one image to another in rapid succession.

"Stay close." Mother grabbed her hand.

Ghera allowed herself to be led toward a cluster of humans. They had two arms and two legs, but that was where their similarities to her ended. Their eyes were too dark and features too coarse and shoulders too broad. They had thick hair in odd places; some people were missing hair on the tops of their heads, while others had so much hair on their faces, an animal must have attached itself to their mouths like some kind of parasite.

She couldn't interpret the expressions on their faces, and their lack of horns made them seem oddly naked. Humans looked so much like inlaris, which made the differences all the more strange. Ghera shivered as if a *laisha* had crawled across her back.

Then she saw something else: still a human, but much smaller than the others—smaller than even Ghera—holding onto an adult's hand just like she clung to Mother's. The child stared at her, and Ghera stared back. The human had oddly flat skin and no horn nubs at all, but its hand clutched a furry object, small and stuffed. The child—male? female?—spoke to its parent in a language she couldn't understand. Then the strange creature let go of its adult and gazed quizzically at her skin and the nubs of her horns.

It carefully hugged the toy close to its chest for a moment, and then offered it to her with two hands. Ghera looked up at Mother, and, after receiving a nod, touched the object with a tentative hand. It felt soft, comforting, and very familiar—almost as if her stuffed *khima* had returned to reassure her.

"Jey-nee." The human child said the word and pointed to itself, then motioned to Ghera. When she didn't answer, the human pointed to other objects around them and said words in a language Ghera didn't understand. "Gar-bej-can. Fai-yer-hai-drent. Khaar." She then pointed at herself again. "Jey-nee."

Ghera beamed with understanding. She put her hand on her chest in a sign of introduction. "Ghera."

In that moment, Trenar and her inhabitants weren't so strange. Despite the fact that Ghera didn't know English and Jey-nee spoke no Anshahar, they had communicated in a language that was truly universal: the language of peace, the language of understanding, and the language of connection.

A TALE OF TWO MOONS

WOELF DIETRICH

26 YEARS AFC

I MISS MY WORLD. Two large moons loomed over our little planet. One was white, the other bright ube. At night, when no cloud could be seen and their orbital paths crossed, they seemed to make love. Their auras touched in a dance of exquisite poetry, splashing our landscapes with hues of pale purple. I used to stare at them until my eyes burned. Theirs was the story of our creation, of our planet Inlarah as it orbited the great star, Inlar.

I miss my world. Our star so warm and gentle, hardly changing during our planet's two seasons. Our crops never failed. We had no droughts. Our rain fell soft and gentle like a mother's caress. Our sun so comforting and consistent. So protective, like a lover's embrace. Not like Earth.

I abhor Earth. A world of extremes and contrasts seemingly at war with itself. Misery permeates the planet like pus oozing from infected pores. Its very fabric is sodden with despair. Oh, how I loathe humans and their strange and barbaric customs. They come across as so entitled when, in truth, they are no more advanced than those violent *bundr-ah*. At least *bundr-ah* know their place, but then, they would, wouldn't they? They called Inlarah home, too.

On Inlarah, there had been order; our expectations were curbed by our respective roles and duties. Not like here. On Inlarah, I was Elite. My family owned vast estates. I could trace my ancestry back to when the first star's children burst into being, when they spawned the planets and populated them with their essence. Yes, in me burns the life force of the greatest and oldest star in our galaxy, and yet here I am, forced to scrub floors in human latrines like some common slave, having the smell of their waste on me, day after day.

I long for my world.

I long for a phantom. A ghost. I long for something that doesn't exist. My world is gone. Nothing is left. Just a blackness, an empty space where not even stars deign to shine. May it forever live in my memory and console me on lonely nights.

And the evil thing that stole our planet? The thing that is both enemy and creator to our great star? It's coming to Earth next. There is no escaping its reach. No matter where we go. Wickedness hunts us, hungers for us, without end.

We shall never tell the humans, of course. They already hate us. Why give them more reason? No, we shall plan and prepare and wait. Ours is the story of a species forced to flee, remaining in constant flux. We dare not call any world home because of that looming evil.

Rituals and faith define us. Our practices and norms make us who we are. We should not forget them. They are what it means to be inlari. Our identity is our new home, and we shall cling to our individuality, for it separates us from these barbaric humans, from that thing out there among the distant stars.

My inlari culture is all that I have left now as I wash these filthy floors, the skin on my fingers rough and broken from chemicals and soap.

That, and my sweet memories.

They will do. They have to.

THE CROSSBREED

M.J. KELLEY

SOMETIME AFTER 57 AFC

THE ONLY DOCTOR in town wasn't a doctor at all; she was a nurse. And we all—meaning the people of Elt—took turns volunteering in Shelly's nurse tent. We called that breezy linen a tent. But it was nothing more than old sheets Mr. Fulton had hung up for her. Had a dirt floor like everywhere else. That's where Shelly admitted the woman. Bone-skinny and pregnant, like a balloon on a beanpole, she tripped into the tent, barely able to stand on her own feet. Turned bright red, too, with the labor. No painkillers, so the whole town heard every push like she was dying.

We all knew she was a goner as soon as the thing ripped through with those budding horns and that greenish color on the back of his head. Shelly jumped, almost dropped him. But we did our duty and cleaned the blood and fluid off that green-striped body and that little ridged neck. The mother died a couple hours later. Shows you we weren't meant to breed with them. 'Course

Shelly said the woman dying was unrelated, but what does she know? She's no doctor.

A scattering of old wooden shacks, a few rows of those plastic habitats, one big two-story orphan house, and the flapping bedclothes of Shelly's nurse tent were all there was in Elt. But we didn't mind. Elt's small enough that everybody took care of everybody. But no one wanted to take care of the crossbreed.

Dolten spoke the mind of the town: "Bury the crossbreed with its mother."

But Miss Elliot said, "He deserves at least half the care, him being half human and all."

Dolten didn't argue with her, so the crossbreed went to the orphan house to mix with the human children. Twenty-odd miscreants of all ages scampered 'round the orphan house's dirt-piled yard. In one way or another, laries murdered the parents of all those poor kids.

Folks didn't go there to buy children. It wasn't that kind of place. Miss Elliot cared for them till they could work. And till then, they tramped around mischief-making and idling. Miss Branen said she saw the blond boy and girl roll the crossbreed down a dirt mound into a small hole they dug. That green-backed nibbler wailed so loud when they tried to bury him, Miss Elliot came running. When the little hornhead could crawl, Dave Foster said he saw a girl leading him every which way in the yard with a rope tied about his neck, pulling and yanking and choking him blue—or whatever color they turn.

When he could finally wobble about on his own two feet, he'd strut after the troupe of children as if he were a part of their game, a permanent grin spread between his puffy cheeks, till one of the children would gallop into him, knocking him clear from the play. Dirt-faced and red, he'd sit there howling, tears draining, his prideful little world snatched away.

Couple years after the crossbreed's mother died, the father came 'round. He was a thick-horned one, green on the back of the head, deep ridges in the neck. One ugly son of a bitch. Some say they see nobility in them. People who say that should know better, should go over to Miss Elliot's and look at all the children's faces. People should remember that not all of us come from here. For most, Elt's a home away from home. Except that home we're away from is gone forever. And it's the horned bastards' fault.

The father asked at the nurse tent. Shelly told him, "There's no record of that name here. But a couple years back a woman died from childbirth. Delivered the crossbreed myself."

Sun had escaped the sky by then, and the father went from habitation to habitation asking after shelter. No laries allowed in human homes. Not here. He slept in the dirt that night.

Next day, he went to the orphan house and said in that broken, fluty English they have, "My son?"

Miss Elliot stood in the doorway. "Nothing's for free," she told him. "I expect to be paid for the care I give."

"And if I'd never found him?"

"That fancy larie tech you got will do."

"I have nothing."

Miss Elliot's no dummy. We all knew that. She waved him away as if to say, Shoo!

"Genetic test," he told her. "I'll prove he's mine."

But when he reappeared at Shelly's tent, she wouldn't give him time of day with a test. He marched back to the orphan house. This time the whole town came out to witness. He spoke real quiet to Miss Elliot. Then she slammed the door on him, showed him laries can't just come and demand things. That woman is brave as they come. The father left after that.

A few weeks later, figures appeared on the ridge. A patrol? One of ours? No patrols on Tuesdays. When they got closer, we saw their horned heads, and we got ready. Armed ourselves—men, women, and children.

The laries marched right up to the orphan house like they owned the place, like they owned our town. We formed up, surrounding them.

Miss Elliot said, "If you take the crossbreed without paying so much as a battery, you're liable for a war."

"Give us the child, and we'll leave," a big one said.

"They want a fight. We'll fight." Mr. Dolten pointed his rifle at the gaggle of laries.

"Wait." The father held up a cube glinting in the sun. One of those larie batteries that never loses its charge.

"Deal." Miss Elliot gestured for him to come in, like the father was a guest.

Miss Elliot said they walked back to the nursery and found the crossbreed hanging from a doorknob, one of those makeshift leashes 'round his neck, that human face scrunched to the middle like he'd tottered into some kind of anguishing sleep.

"He'd been dead thirty minutes at least," Miss Elliot told us later. "Still don't know which child done him in. But thought I was about to join the nibbler when the father untied the knot 'round his neck. I tell you, he must've seen the shock on my face, or I'd be at death's door."

The father returned to the larie outfit without saying a word. We all thought they'd try to burn the town. Instead, they made Shelly tell them where the mother was buried. No gravestone for her. Her body was with the rest of the dead out where we dumped the refuse. The father carried the limp crossbreed to the bone yard and performed some ritual when the stars began to blink. Some of us went out there to watch. Dolten said he couldn't tell if the laries sang or spoke, but that lilting hullabaloo wasn't like any singing he'd ever heard. Most of us stayed home hoping they'd get the hell out. Eventually they did. They took the crossbreed's body with them.

A NEW EARTH

DANA LEIPOLD

15 YEARS AFC

THERE IS SOMETHING about how they walk—no, glide—into a room that makes you feel as if a great source of wisdom has just graced you with its presence. The way they hold you with their violet eyes like a precious treasure, their voices like a long-forgotten song. They'll tell you that we gave them a home after their celestial flight, and they are the ones who should be eternally grateful to us—but I say we have benefitted the most from them.

When I was a young child, we had big problems, and it seemed that no one had the solutions. We had all but given up, thinking we were alone in the universe, and we had screwed up our planet pretty bad. In our moment of greatest need, they appeared with their energy cubes and planet-cleaning technology like galactic angels.

I'll never forget the first time I shook hands with one of them. His hands were soft, like suede, and unexpectedly warm. Since their skin is iridescent, you tend to think they run cold, like a reptile, but that wasn't the case. I tried to pronounce his name, but I'm sure I must've sounded like an idiot, "E-roo-veer."

Of course, he said mine perfectly.

"Paul Agoston, pleased to make your acquaintance."

He bowed his head while I stammered.

"Nice to...I think I said your name wrong. Sorry."

"You were not completely incorrect." He smiled. "It is Limstile Eh-rou-veer, or you can call me Lim, which is much easier."

We laughed. Another unexpected surprise because I'd heard that they sounded like neighing horses when they laugh, but Lim sounded more like a chattering squirrel.

He and I shared the same responsibilities as scientists, but, of course, in two completely different worlds. We were part of a special team gathered by the United Nations Space Exploration Program, or UNSEP as it's commonly known, to encourage "knowledge sharing" between us and them. My job involved testing new compounds for use in space stations that could withstand extreme ranges in temperature and velocity, especially during entry into various planetary atmospheric conditions. Although I'd just worked on a project using a Martian material with promising results, I was eager to talk with Lim about quartillium. From what I had heard, it was unlike any compound we'd ever worked with before.

"I've heard a lot about your work. When you see where we're at, you'll likely think you've gone back to the Pleistocene Epoch."

Lim stared at me, his forehead furrowed as if he were trying to solve a complex problem; his horns, thick and textured, gave him the appearance of a noble ram.

"I'm sorry; I don't understand."

"Oh! No, I'm sorry." I chuckled. "Human scientist joke."

"Joke?" He repeated.

Whenever I get nervous, I say dumb things, and I'd assumed they knew more than we did about everything, including my scientifically accurate reference to the time humans appeared on Earth. I'd also assumed that they had a sense of humor, but they'd been on Earth for only a short period of time. So maybe some things about us humans were harder to pick up than others?

"Yes, something said that usually elicits amusement or laughter, but in my case, I choked."

"Do you need medical assistance?" He patted my back with a look of concern. "I know the human anatomy very well and can perform a quick maneuver that will clear your esophagus or larynx if needed."

By this time, I actually *was* choking because of the absurdity. I couldn't stop laughing as he tried to give me a bizarre version of the Heimlich maneuver. We were face-to-face, his arms were around my torso and he instructed me to lift my arms in the air and bend over backward. After a few seconds of this, I caught my breath long enough to get words out of my mouth.

"Really, I'm okay. I can breathe."

He released me with a huge smile.

"Good, because the joke is on you."

Then he threw his head back and erupted into loud squirrel chatter, almost losing his balance. His laugh was so contagious, I joined him.

Once we regained our composure, we got to work.

LEAVING CHICAGO

ELAINE CHAO

40 YEARS AFC

ISHAK PULLED THE family gravsled into the lot at Kauffman's, adjusted her horn beads, checked her comm for the grocery list, and tried to put herself into a zen frame of mind. The argument with Balmish that morning had rattled her more than she had let on at the time.

"Why can't you get your horns out of the sand, Mishak?" he had hissed quietly, pulling his coat on as he prepared to walk the kids to their elementary school. "Don't think that we're safe just because Mikkol and Akhana haven't been injured yet."

Some stubborn part of her wanted to be sure that moving to New Zealand was the right thing to do. Other inlaris from the Chicago area had left already, of course, most right after the death of an inlari teen in one of the Westchester high schools and that disastrous Blackhawks game where four inlari fans had been corralled, beaten, and almost hanged.

But Mishak had been born in Chicago, and the place permeated her soul. She had grown up on deep dish and had walked through the gray brick buildings at the UChicago campus as an undergrad. She had attended more than her share of Cubs games and had helped put on her high school's homecoming dance. In some ways, she felt more human than inlari, thinking of all of these human places as home, eating human food, and partaking in human traditions. Her parents had thrown themselves into human culture to help them relate to their coworkers, and Mishak had followed in their example, discovering that she resonated so much more with human culture than inlari.

Who cared that humans were unhappy that the inlari leadership meted out their technology at a slow pace to their allies? It wasn't as if *Mishak* had any control over that, and she *certainly* didn't have any technology that wasn't available on the market. No, everything she owned would have passed in any human household, right down to the battered forks and spoons she had purchased in a secondhand store as a graduate student in Michigan. After all, it wasn't like anyone had actually been injured in her town or in her neighborhood. Westchester was on the other side of the greater Chicago area, and none of the inlaris in her area had reported any problems.

Mishak pressed her finger against the cart to engage its silent antigrav field, tethered it to her wrist, and began her trek through the familiar grocery store. She'd been to Kauffman's weekly since they had purchased their home a mile away, and it was well stocked with everything a suburban American family would need. She tagged apples and a variety of vegetables for addition to the gravcart, cruised through the dairy and bread section, stopping briefly for those toaster pastry things that Mikkol seemed to crave.

Then she headed for the international aisle. One of her deals with Balmish was that he got at least *one* inlari meal a week, if only to satisfy a certain nostalgia and to instill some kind of cultural pride in their children. While Kauffman's had only two different brands of the *urshil* paste she needed for *kipshal*, it did have her preferred one. She could easily buy what she needed at her local grocery store instead of trekking all the way across town to the nearest inlari store, where everything was labeled in the dizzying Anshahar script and the smell of *ikasha* incense permeated every corner.

Mishak reached up for the jar just as her gravcart crashed into her hip, causing a frisson of pain to shoot up her side. The gravcarts were programmed to avoid collisions, which meant that someone had intentionally bumped against it.

A young woman in a purple Northwestern sweatshirt sullenly glared at Mishak as she passed. The human pulled her gravcart down the wide aisle, her springy ponytail swishing as she walked.

Mishak was taken aback at the offense. No apology, no explanation of the impact? She felt grateful the gravcart's technology prevented more serious bodily injury, but was unsure what to make of the situation. Should she let it go or confront the woman? In that moment of indecision, the other woman disappeared into another aisle.

Mishak resolved to put the incident out of her mind, turned the corner, and headed down the breakfast aisle, stopping in front of her family's favorite breakfast manufacturer's slot. Images of the boxes cycled vertically, and all she had to do was make her selections with a few quick touches to have them added to her gravcart. Halfway down the aisle, a human in her late thirties pointedly ignored her; her two children—upper elementary school, by the look of them—had no such manners. One child cupped his hands behind his head like horns, his fingers splayed wide, while the other laughed loudly at his brother's antics. The mother said nothing.

Mishak's stomach sank as she realized that the mother had no interest in correcting her children's behavior. She hurriedly pulled her cart out of the aisle. *Boys will be boys*, she reassured herself, but the words rang hollow. How long had she glossed over similar incidents in the past and simply blamed it on societal norms?

She pulled the gravcart toward the checkout counter and spotted an elderly inlari next to it, picking up what looked like a broken jar of pickles. He was thin, his horns weathered with age, but he carefully sorted the glass into the bin. Mishak wondered why they didn't have the autocleaners do that, but Kauffman's valued the personal touch and often tried to invoke that retro vibe in its stores.

"What the hell, Walter," the checker complained. She was a woman in her late forties, her frizzy hair pulled into a messy bun at the top of her head. "Why d'you have to be so slow?"

She glanced up to see Mishak and twisted her mouth in disgust. "Well, come on over here," she said. "Mind the wet spot. Walter there ain't too fast with the cleanup."

Walter stood up slowly, his thin limbs unfolding in a manner that pained Mishak to watch. When he stood, his eyes met hers with vulnerability in their violet depths. She hadn't seen him before, but she sensed that he had been beaten down by time, circumstances, and repeated humiliation by those around him. His badge said his name was "Valshik."

The checker loaded Mishak's food so that the apples were bruised and cereal was crushed, and both tumbled to smash the egg carton in the gravcart by the time she got back to the 'sled. She was numb as she unloaded the cart of groceries, adjusting the food so that the bruised apples and cracked eggs rested on top.

Mishak crawled into the gravsled and gripped the steering wheel so hard her hands shook. Then she was the one who shook, her emotions roiling like pent-up lava, with a turbulent intensity that made her feel like vomiting.

It had been so easy to think her family would be exempt, that she would be safe because she had lived in the midst of a multicultural bubble. The signs had been there the entire time; what she had dismissed as childish pranks or mere irritability had been a pattern of anger that had boiled over into violence. Her hope and optimism for a better future evaporated like the ephemeral illusion it had been.

Balmish was right.

It was time to leave.

THE DAY THE SKY BURNED

WOELF DIETRICH

51 YEARS AFC

THE GREAT INLARI War broke out on my eleventh birthday. On that day, I saw the sky burn. I had been feeding our chickens in the coop when a thunderous crack shredded the early morning calm, sending the chickens fluttering and flapping wildly. Dropping the feed bowl, I ran for cover in my family home as another explosion ripped through the air above me. Intense heat swathed my skin, like I had stumbled into a furnace.

The day before, Pa had told us the governments were talking about peace. Conflict between the aliens and humans had been escalating for months, and people were talking about a looming war. He said the aliens didn't want to fight. Only wanted to live unharmed and peacefully, but the Russians weren't interested.

And then the fire in the sky happened.

I was midway to the farmhouse when I saw Pa wrenching open the back door. I wanted to shout, but my words froze in my throat as a molten ball of blue fire engulfed our home. Not so much an explosion as an incandescent implosion that reduced the structure to smoldering rubble.

The shock wave hurled me backwards a ways, and I landed on my back in the tall Oklahoma grass. I stared up at the sky, gazing into a crimson hell where hundreds of fiery pillars crisscrossed, leaving trails of smoke and falling debris. The earth shook under me as if some giant beast had woken and was now clawing its way through the crust.

I cried, stunned by what had happened to my family—what was happening to my world. I stayed on my back, tears streaming down my face as the world burned around me. Smoke and sulfur filled my nose and mouth and burned like acid inside me, but I didn't care. Sorrow and fear consumed me completely, leaving no space for physical pain.

Finally, the sun exploded into a million shards of light and molten vapor, and my eyes melted from their sockets.

I would never cry again.

A SAR team found me two days later. I had burns over seventy percent of my body. According to them, I was lucky to be alive. Naked agony tore at every fiber of my being. Tubes snaked into my mouth and nose and veins, giving me oxygen, feeding me nutrients, expelling rotten liquids from my mutilated body.

They told me I was heading to Australia. Better medical facilities there, they said. Nothing could be done for my sight, of course, but I was alive, which was better than being dead. If I'd still had a tongue, I would have argued that point.

They told me Australia held the last vestige of hope for humans. That I would be safe there.

Safe from whom? I wondered.

THE CAMPAIGN

M.J. KELLEY

44 YEARS AFC

H E KNEW WHERE Adanna lived because he followed her home from work most nights. He watched her from a building parallel to her apartment's high rise. Her home resided in the sky, far above the city of Boleez on the East side of South Island, New Zealand. Sometimes, clouds passed below her silver tower, obscuring her from view. In the mornings, he waited for her to leave, and he followed her to the office where she worked for Dolsum, Becker, & Waters—the advertising firm helping to usher in the new inlari-human future, promoting collaboratively built, self-sustaining super cities like Boleez, Tiro, and Naven.

Adanna's inlari mother died in childbirth. Adanna grew up in Africa until she was eleven, and then her human father sent her to New Zealand to live with her great aunt, whom the family called "Nana." During her time in Africa, the city of Sandal was being constructed by inlari-human collaboration, the first of its kind. She dreamed of the day when she'd live in those towers, of the day when she'd contribute to creating such a place. He knew this because he'd impersonated a journalist and interviewed playmates from her childhood, as well as old friends and family members. He befriended her ex-lovers and even found her father in an abandoned shack outside Nairobi.

When he needed sleep, his partners, Dan and Janine, watched Adanna.

He studied her advertising campaigns. Her commercials and ads played on his eyes, painted over reality by means of his optical implants. Laughing and smiling families of all species, even half-breeds like him—the bane of the world—formed interspecies families. Fluid super cities rose in 3D-models around him, playing combinations of music, the style and symbol never subtle...

She produced documentaries. Her firm funded movies and media of all types to penetrate the world's prejudices and re-form them into awareness about the possibilities the two species could enjoy. She was on the front lines, fighting the battle against a world turned sour on the inlari—the aliens' welcome had run out. Countries actively deported them, along with the hybrids, to New Zealand and Australia, who awaited them with open arms. It was no wonder: the increased inlari population stimulated economic growth, so the GDP of both countries increased.

In other commercials, a father danced with his daughter in an evergreen pasture, a hiking trio of hybrids summited a tall mountain and came upon the cloud-encrusted skyline of Boleez, while an air frigate and a lancer cruised along in the foreground revealing the site of Saffron, the new Australian super city. He watched documentaries on the food plants and maintenance centers, featuring these cities' self-sustainability. Eliza Watanabe and Timothy Rafeallo, the first humans to warp-jump and spend any significant time with the aliens, spoke in sound bites and brief interviews about the benefits of collaboration.

Her films and shows and movies and eyelid banners and books—a propaganda maelstrom. They even exported the smells of super cities, bottled air and fragrance samples in nugget-like tubes you could fit into your nostril while you watched the advertisements. These ads and ideas flashed around the world, strategically placed for maximum effect.

Many credited Adanna and her firm for opening the floodgates to Australia and New Zealand. Power. Money. And, over the years, the world's brain trust all flowed south, making these two countries the premier cultural and technological centers of Earth. The key component to this shift was an ideological advertising executive—Adanna.

When a recruiter contacted him on behalf of a third party who wished to remain anonymous, he knew what they wanted. This wasn't a misinformation operation or a simple recon. He was to deliver a message to the inlari-human clients of Adanna's firm, the same ones bankrolling a new world order and the new city civilizations sprouting all over the island nations.

They wanted her dead.

ON TUESDAY, A SECRET ADMIRER SENT HER A WHITE KITTEN. HE was the delivery man, from Gift Emporium of South Island, a company that existed only in digital records. There was no secret admirer.

"I didn't know companies still hand-delivered things," she said, flustered. She blushed when reading the card—he knew she would. He surmised that she didn't want to accept the gift, but her heart always intervened. He knew this about her. Knew she liked the idea of someone thinking of her.

A surgical implant inside the cat would transmit audio. They watched her, and now they could listen, too.

Nana died a few weeks later. The wake took place at the Dolsum, Becker, Waters senior partner's home. Guests sat in chairs on a large veranda overlooking the endless snow-capped mountains and fields at the city's edge.

He wore black to the funeral, Janine at his side, posing as his wife.

Afterwards, he pulled Janine toward the exit. Someone grabbed his elbow.

"You're a delivery man, aren't you?" Adanna stood beside him. "Almost didn't recognize you with the beard you've grown. How'd you know Nana?"

"Busted." Dan's voice rang in ear speakers.

"I tended to her garden and the dogs when Thatcher was out of town. Helped with her chores." And now for the big risk: "I was there the first time she fell."

Guilt surfaced on Adanna's face, hurt revealing itself for a moment. He'd guessed right. The first year Nana got sick, Adanna had been too busy to see her—all those advertising campaigns for new cities, for the new future in New Zealand and Australia.

She composed herself and smiled. "Yes, of course. You must think I'm so rude. She would've loved to know you were here. Thank you for coming."

"My deepest condolences for your loss," Janine said, tugging on his arm.

"You're a hybrid?" Adanna asked.

This time he must have looked shocked. He'd had plastic surgery, his horns removed and his skin dyed a dark pigment. Most didn't know, didn't suspect. He changed his identity often, repressing his personal history. He became his work. He was his work. Perhaps she had a memory for faces and an intuition for people like his own: he could always spot a hybrid in a crowd.

"Hybrids should stick together." She smiled.

He nodded and then left, the sting of her words reverberating inside him. She'd unknowingly hit a nerve, but he'd allowed it to happen.

She knew nothing about him.

After that, he didn't watch her anymore. He'd been marked. So he logged into her private messages, and into all her family's scan bars and slates, and loaded thousands of pictures of Adanna into his eye implants.

"Now I can watch you anytime I want."

He found himself pretending Adanna was a friend. Imagined reveries entered his mind, daydreams cresting on waves of tedium as he flipped through her pictures. He allowed himself these fantasies, while knowing such a decision was a dangerous mental compromise. He'd been making such bargains the last few years; with his personality and emotions manipulated and suppressed for so long, his mind seemed to be rebelling, inviting these unbidden lapses in control.

He knew it would work, though Janine and Dan hated the idea.

"Too many variables."

"Too many things can go wrong."

Eventually, he wore them down, agreeing to pay their fees out of pocket if the operation failed.

"What about you?" Dan asked. "If we fail, our employers will come after you for their money."

"Maybe."

"Human purists pay well, but they're lethal bastards." Janine bit her nail.

"Our employers aren't necessarily human. Both species have purist groups," he said. "Anytime you sell peace and prosperity—"

"Stop right there," Janine said. "No good comes from worrying about politics."

He smiled. "Yet we're a weapon of politics—"

Janine covered her ears. "La la la—not listening."

The next day, he sat himself in Adanna's favorite cafe, the one she frequented every morning.

She recognized him immediately, but he pretended not to see her.

"Hey there," she said. "You live in the neighborhood?"

"Passing through."

"You want to get coffee sometime? Talk about Nana?"

They exchanged contact numbers.

They met four times for coffee before she invited him up. He thought her lovely. Always had. Her work was brilliant, and many people didn't understand her genius.

They didn't know her like he did.

He and Adanna made love on her wide sofa, and she made him jasmine tea afterward.

"You filthy bastard, Feldon. I can't believe you—" He blinked off his earpiece, and Janine's voice disappeared. Then he put the kitten out on the porch and closed the glass sliding door.

While Adanna showered, he grabbed her company scan bar, connected it to one that looked identical and copied all her info on to it. He now had her life's work, all the proprietary information from her firm. And she had a special virus. Dan had assured him that, when she plugged it in at her office, it would set off a chain reaction, igniting everyone's internal implants, killing most people and paralyzing the rest.

He looked at the lethal scan bar and hesitated for a moment. Then he placed it where she had left the original.

The next morning, they exited together and got coffee at the cafe. She hadn't stopped smiling. "Why'd you have your horns removed?" She beamed.

"A story for another time," he teased.

They said their goodbyes at the fountains, and he watched her, as he often had, cross the square to her office building. "Tell me when she plugs in the scan bar," he said to Dan, who was listening remotely.

He'd call her after she plugged it in and get her out of the building.

After an hour or so, he got tired of pacing, and sat on the wide steps down near the statues in the square. Something hit him in the head, hard. He jumped to his feet to find Adanna.

On the ground near his feet was the scan bar. He quickly blinked three times to disconnect Dan and Janine.

"Who are you?" Her words hung in the air between them like an echo in a cave. Her face had furrowed. She'd developed bags under her eyes he hadn't noticed before. The pain of his betrayal shook her, yet he saw hope—or sensed it somehow. She was giving him a chance to explain.

But his mistake had been made a long time ago, long before he ever knew Adanna.

He picked up the scan bar, the viral implant bomb, and placed it in his pocket.

"I'm sorry." The words fell from his mouth, but they had no force, no weight to them. It was the apology of a man whose mental resources had momentarily vanished, no longer able to support the falsehood of himself and his place in this world.

Then he turned and ran.

HE WATCHED ADANNA IN HER APARTMENT. HE FOLLOWED HER home from work, waited for her in the mornings. He had inlari tattoos needled into his arms. And he had short horns implanted on his skull where his old ones had been. He deposited the money, his own, into Janine and Dan's accounts, as he'd promised. And he returned his employer's payment in full, hoping that would suffice to keep him alive. When she went out on a date, met with friends, attended the opera, or the inlari symphonic performances, he was there—watching. Ensuring she'd always be safe. Ensuring no one like him would ever get close to her again.

THE BERSERKER'S CODE

WOELF DIETRICH

90 YEARS AFC

THE BERSERKER SAT there in the blood-caked dust, gasping, nostrils flaring wildly, vacuuming barrels of air into his massive chest. Huge yellow tusks jutted from his thick lower lip, contorting his face into a permanent scowl. Gnarled stumps for fingers curled around the handle of an ugly cleaver, while his eyes spat hate-filled venom. His other hand tried to stanch the life flowing from his ruined leg. If he felt any pain, he didn't show it. These orc-looking aliens were tough assholes. And massive—like humanoid rhinos. At seven feet, they were regular hulks.

The inlari officer fled after we'd decimated his band of berserkers. We intercepted the raiding party between the beach and Farcord's farm. Intel had been good on this one.

But, damn, they were brutal fighters. Though we ambushed them, they ripped through us like we were paper soldiers. We kept pushing. Hard. Our training and discipline helped, enough at least to kill three of the berserkers and chase off the inlari officer who had dropped his blaster when I'd shot him in the chest. Only his armor had saved him.

But they killed four of my men. Good soldiers with family back home. Now it was just me and the one surviving berserker and the inlari officer's blaster.

"Yer an ugly bastard, ain't ya?" I eyed him with a mixture of hate and anger and some relief.

He didn't reply. Just glared at me as I climbed slowly to my feet. Earlier the point of his cleaver had ripped a line clean across my chest, splitting my battle jacket and shirt, parting the skin down to the bone. My chest felt like someone poured lava over the flesh.

I still wasn't sure how I'd managed it, but in the split second it would've taken him to finish the job, I'd somehow brought up my stolen blaster and turned his kneecap to bloody mush.

And so here we were, two bleeding enemies staring at each other, seething with barely containable hate.

"Thought you had me there for a second, didn't you?"

A short grunt came from his lips as he eyed me. I picked up what was left of my railgun. The metal parts were twisted, and the polymer parts melted. I tossed it.

The blaster still had enough charge for one more shot, so I could kill the alien now. Only I didn't want to. Not yet anyway.

"Do you understand English?" I studied his face and his small bloodshot eyes for a reaction. "I think you do." No reaction. He had a dainty nose and weird runtish ears. He would've been funny-looking if he wasn't so damn intimidating.

"Come on. Say something, you bastard."

Scraping the blade across the gravel he lifted it and brought it down with a dull thud and grunted again. The meaning was clear.

"Yeah? Fuck you too."

My chest burned, but I couldn't attend it without neutralizing this animal first. He was far from harmless, despite his wounds.

The lower part of his massive leg lay twisted at an odd angle, and, where his knee used to be, only strings of flesh and cartilage remained. Blood pooled under his ruined limb. He might die soon from blood loss anyway.

We were the only ones left breathing. Bodies of the fallen littered the graveled sand around us, soaking the ground with human and alien blood. I'd lost mates before, and it doesn't get any easier. You learn to disconnect from that side of your brain when death takes your friends and brothers-in-arms. Back at base, I'd take time to connect with that part again—for a moment only, that is. Any longer, and I'd be looking for trouble. That amount of pain and loss does a soldier no good. Even now, thinking about it caused my throat to thicken and swell with building emotion. So I reached for my anger and allowed it to shape the building emotion, to control it. Refocus it. I'd always been good at focusing my anger.

I studied the alien's energy pistol in my hand, and for a moment, the urge to shoot the surviving berserker in the face for the stolen lives of my brothers, overwhelmed me. I struggled to regain control, and I felt a tremor go down my arm as I squeezed the butt of the pistol.

He must have been able to sense my thoughts because he had a grotesque grin on his face.

He would welcome death. Of course he would. That was the berserker way. They lived to die in battle. They never ran from a fight unless ordered to by their inlari masters.

"What's your name, huh?" I walked closer but made sure I stayed out of his reach, should he attempt a lunge.

"They must call you something. I want to know your name before I kill you."

He grunted again, this time more earnest, and again, he hit the ground with the cleaver, sending grit flying.

"Naw, it ain't gonna be that easy, mate. I want you to speak. I want you to tell me your name. You've been on this planet long enough."

The berserker squinted at me, his bushy brow knotting above his nose, and again plowed the ground with his cleaver.

"Tell you what: I'll give you a quick death." I pointed to the blaster. "But you'll need to give me your name. If you don't, I'll shoot off your other leg and leave you here for the dingos to eat. Decide quickly."

I stood up and aimed the blaster at his other leg, waiting for him to decide.

The berserker lunged at me, the cleaver slicing empty air in front of me as I jumped back. His momentum carried him forward, and he fell face first into the gravel, one hand still gripping his thigh, while the other held onto the weapon.

Without thinking, I squeezed the trigger. The plasma blast took his hand, leaving vapor and a melted cleaver's handle.

The berserker gave a balking roar as he pulled his mutilated stump of an arm to his chest and curled into a ball.

I discarded the useless blaster. I just had my old 9mm Browning on my hip, but it would have to do.

I should kill him. No sense in dragging out his pain. I didn't really want to torture him or make him suffer. He was just a soldier like me, doing his master's bidding. I didn't like the inlaris, but the berserkers with their primal nature and brutal ways followed a code I could at least respect. They didn't run from a fight, and they were brave. For whatever that is worth. This guy didn't deserve to go this way.

I pulled out the browning, clicked off the safety, and aimed at his head.

Then he threw sand in my face.

The Browning bucked in my hand, but I was blind and didn't see if I hit him, and then he slammed against me, gouging my chest with his tusks. His weight drove the air from my lungs and pinned me to the ground. One of the tusks ripped a gash open along the side of my ribcage while he smashed his elbow into my face. I had my tactical helmet on, which took the brunt of the force, but his elbow shots still rocked me. I tasted blood. If this continued, he'd kill me. Even wounded and mutilated, the berserker's strength and mass alone overpowered me.

I tried to aim the Browning but the berserker clamped his maw over my wrist and snapped the bone. I yelled and dropped the pistol.

With renewed panic, I squirmed and tried to worm myself out from under him, but it was useless. He weighed a ton.

With his good arm, the alien tried to strangle me, his thick fingers pushing my head back as he tried to secure his hold.

My left arm was still free, and I frantically searched for the tactical knife sheathed on my battle vest.

The berserker's fingers finally found their mark, and he squeezed. My air supply stopped abruptly. He kept squeezing, and a sharp, needle-like stab of pain shot down my back. My eyes felt like they were bulging, and the world became a thick fog. My fingers located the knife, the familiar contours of the handle giving me a spark of hope.

I pulled the knife and plunged it into the berserker's face, the point penetrating the corner of his right eye at an angle. My blade went in deep.

His great body shuddered, and the last thing I remember was a gurgling sound.

Then I passed out.

AFTER A RESCUE PARTY FOUND ME, THEY TOOK ME TO A NEARBY farm where someone's grandmother nursed me back to health. I often think about that day with the berserker. If he'd wanted to, he could easily have killed me with the first of his elbow blows. He certainly could have torn my head off, injuries or not. And squeezing my neck the way he did...like he wanted to give me time to fight back. The berserker knew he was dying, and he wanted a warrior's way out. He went out fighting. This code may make them utterly ruthless, but they're also the naivest in this war between the species. And maybe the noblest.

My soldier's heart understood and respected the code. I've got no family left. They were taken from me many years ago. Just another statistic in this ongoing conflict with the aliens. Battling the inlaris and their barbarian hordes is what I live for. Have been living for, for a long time. The berserker was a harbinger of my own lot in this mess. I too am destined to bleed out in the red dust of this land one day.

The thought of it did not frighten me. Instead, a slow peace fell over me and I embraced it.

LOCAR'S DESTINY

DANA LEIPOLD

121 YEARS BFC – PLANET NARU

*I*T'S NOT POSSIBLE. *Since I can remember, everyone in my family has belonged to the highest caste, nodour. We have been responsible for upholding the way of the Great Star, taking us through millennia of hardships, and furthering our technological discoveries. Why did I get this result? I know, as soon as I open this door, they will ask me. They will want to know.*

MY MOTHER STANDS AT THE WINDOW, ARMS BEHIND HER BACK, hands clasped. She's gazing at the city's spires silhouetted against the purple horizon—a peaceful sight if it weren't for the massive rush of skycrafts jetting by.

She turns to me, and her face holds an expectation that weighs on me like an unwanted burden. Her mouth moves, and I hold up my hand. She tilts her head, and the ends of her curving horns catch the light.

"I know what you're going to ask me."

Father enters from the corridor, his lean arms open. "Locar!"

We embrace, and then he motions to the seats by the window. He puts his hand on my mother's waist, guiding her to sit beside him. I sit across from them and notice that my father's long face, framed by his intricate lattice of horns, beams with anticipation.

"So? Technology, right? You keep telling me how close we're getting to space-time warping." He smiles at my mother who stares at me, piercing my thoughts.

I can't delay any longer.

"I am *tade*."

They both gasp.

"How?" One of them asks; I'm not sure which.

As if I know. I've been preparing for the *Menktun* my entire life, just like any other youngling, since this test determines what role we perform in society. But I never expected this.

My throat is drier than the Drandis Desert. I squeak out, "I don't know."

My mother reaches for my knee, and then her hand lingers there.

"This can't be right." My father bolts up and paces the floor. "No one ever tests below their caste. There have been some who test above, but that's very rare."

"The *Menktun* is never wrong." Her eyes fill with tears as she scans my face. "But my son is not a *tade* soldier. You are meant for something better."

She touches my cheek, and I want to say something, but my mouth won't form the words. All I can think of is the grueling life that awaits me.

"I need to contact the *Menktun* commission," he says. "They can be motivated with the right currency." He nods like he's convincing himself.

"Yes, we can fix this," she echoes. "Don't worry, Locar. Everything will be fine."

They both get up and trot to the other room, leaving me with a hollowness I've never felt before. This doesn't feel right. Everything about who we are is based on this test, and it's been that way for millions of years. The fine balance of our caste system works. Who am I to question our way of life? What will happen to my parents if they raise this objection?

I jump from my seat and burst into the communication hub. Luckily, they are still discussing their strategy and haven't made any contacts yet.

"I can't agree to this."

"What are you saying?" My mother looks like she's about to break.

"Maybe there's a reason. There has to be."

"And you're prepared to accept the life assigned to you?" Father asks in a way that feels more like a death sentence than a question.

I find myself nodding, I feel like I'm outside my body.

"You know what that means." Father's eyes plead with me.

"I do."

It means I have to leave my family—and everything I have ever known—to protect and defend the inlari way. I will never have my own family or property. I will become an instrument of the Great Star and do whatever is required of me, even if it means giving up my life.

I take my pendant, the family crest I've worn since I was eight years old, and set it on the credenza. I remember the day my father gave it to me—I'd just finished my apprenticeship for technological engineering.

"Locar, please." Mother grabs my arms, shaking me, and I allow it because this will be the last time I see her. When she stops, I touch her face, trying to memorize the contours.

We realize my father is gone about the same time.

"He didn't go to the commission. Did he?"

Before she can answer, I'm running out the door. I only hope I can stop him.

HORN MAN

M.J. KELLEY

83 YEARS AFC

THEY CALLED WALKER the Horn Man because twenty years ago he hunted laries and chopped off their horns. Large horns, spiraling horns, upturned tusk-like horns, baby spikes, curling horns like that of a ram. He took 'em all. He earned the nickname around the time he welded two big horns, white as pearl, onto the hood of an old topless jeep. I didn't know him then, but I'd heard the stories.

About six years before Walker's horn hunting—near the end of the Great War—Sheldon Walker was just north of town, with the Queensland Home Defense Militia. The battalion landed there, large carrier ships dropping laries by the hundreds at the water's edge. The militia hid in the tree line as the laries waded onto the beach, their bodies moving en masse, like a serpent ebbing sideways up the sand at them. Snapper rifles pulsed as the carriers jetted away, and Walker opened fire. His mate Charlie took shrapnel to the head and fell inert next to him. Explosions and blasts lit up the beach, and, over the ocean, faraway ignitions of white signaled the start to the Battle of the Coral Sea.

After fending off the larie battalions, Walker returned with the militia to Beachmere to find its ashen remains. An enemy unit or two must've slipped by them somehow or landed closer to town, unleashing havoc. Swirling black smoke thickened the air. His lungs struggled, and his eyes stung. He searched for his home along the decimated streets, all his reference points turned to blackened rubble.

The laries had flame blasted his house. He found his children's bones in the rubble, stained black from the flames, their bones mixed in with the larger ones of his wife, Helena. He pushed his family's bones around in the soot and waited for tears, for pain.

Nothing came.

Instead, Walker felt outside himself, as if sitting in an emotionless void, a thick soup between him and the world. A growing tension constricted his muscles. Sour acid accumulated in his intestines, burning up into his throat. He found himself cringing and massaging his chest. He felt sick. And then, frothing around in him, a deliberate rage soaked into his skin, festering within him, snapping his awareness back inside his body.

WITH HAMMERS AND TIMBER AND WIRE AND NAILS, WALKER helped rebuild Beachmere, home by home. The world beyond Australia and New Zealand was mostly gone, and so industry slowed all around him. When the work dried up in town, Walker trudged a few miles in the hot sun to Brisbane and stood for hours in crowded labor lines. He watched people siphon fuel from gas stations and dismantle cars and machines for their power cubes.

He suspected elite inlaris and humans hoarded the precious cubes, as beef and other goods became harder and more expensive to transport from the interior, and mining operations halted. Refugees drowned Brisbane; humans and inlaris alike searched for work and waited in the labor lines. Soon, the Australian government released all the inlari soldiers who had tried to invade the country in the last days of the Great War. They mixed with the Aussie-born laries until Walker couldn't tell the difference. Seeing aliens in the labor lines ahead of him made him think of his dead family, and adrenaline surged through his veins. The physically bigger inlaris always got chosen for construction work before him.

Injustice fumed inside him, and, at night before bed, he imagined killing inlaris brutally with knives and rifles, and these fantasies racked his body with tension, each projection encasing his sorrow, burying it deeper and deeper.

He felt the tension, saw the growing destitution, a storm front forming, and he sensed it in other humans, too. The laries were too dominant. Australia and New Zealand had won the war that the laries in part started, and although humans and laries had fought on both sides, the war would not have happened at all without the aliens.

He rolled over the timeline in his head: their arrival; their unfair distribution of technology, especially the power cubes that destabilized the world and led to the war; the divisions among the laries that led them to fighting humans and their own kind. The more he thought on it, the more patterns emerged: the laries promised, then broke their promises, disguising their deceit, masking their betrayals.

He recalled the advertisements of his childhood with mixed species families living in high rises among utopian super cities, self-sustainable lies. Now all those cities were gone except Naven, even though he'd fought to protect them, fought on their side. He now saw them for the sham they were, an alien scam that ended in human death and Earth's peril.

He watched the larie gaggles roam Brisbane as he slept in a tent. Watched them make laws, repair buildings with skills he didn't possess. He asked himself every day: *Aren't we just allowing them to do the same thing again?* The human Brisbane politicians didn't see it, and the parliament was being forsaken by alien representation. How could laries know human needs? How could they know what humans had been through?

The injustices accumulated all around him, and he absorbed them like a sponge, his sorrow now shelled in hatred as he watched the silent tempest brew and spread from person to person.

Something was coming. He felt it. Everyone did.

Back then, I felt it, too.

THEN, LIKE THUNDER TO THE TEMPEST, LIKE THE CLARITY OF A storm eye, a voice rose up from the interior, called out from the dust plains and jungles, roused the spirits of the human downtrodden, the weary, the victimized.

"You're not alone," the voice said, starting as a whisper in parapets, at ranches, in community centers and shelters and in fields. The voice belonged to Thaddeus James, a former colonel of the Queensland Home Defense Militia, and soon his voice boomed across the land in pamphlets and small stapled books, and Walker felt the tempest rise, knew change was coming and had it confirmed every time he heard James's voice or read his words. Listening to him, reading him, was as if the raging storm, the confusion of our sorrowful shell, had a voice, had words for the first time. It felt so true, as if the voice came from within, validating our sense of justice.

Walker listened to James on a wide field, alongside hundreds of other people:

"It's not our world anymore. It belongs to the laries. They swindled us with their tech. Killed us in the greatest holocaust the world has ever known. But now it's time to take Earth back. Return the planet to its rightful owners."

Walker cheered with the rest. Cheered and shouted and danced. All the humans around him mad with joy...a primal joy, a liberating joy that finally someone had defined our wrongs and losses. I cheered. And although I didn't know Walker on that day, I watched the crowd swell, the tempest within them, as the voice of Thaddeus James thunderclapped our hearts, and legitimized our fear and anger. "For you, my brothers and sisters, are my human tribe, and we've been gravely wronged..."

Thaddeus James was raising an army. And Walker joined the droves who enlisted.

THEY CALLED HIM THE HORN MAN BECAUSE HE STALKED THE laries and cut off their horns. He rode in an old topless jeep driven by a young, short, emaciated-looking woman from Beachmere who had lost her whole family, too. Her name was Nal. I heard some say Nal was his daughter, and others said she was a lover.

He told me they never slept together. Didn't need to. It was a partnership forged on mutual suffering. They served one another's pain, a bond more ferocious than love, more enticing than sex. She drove, and he shot. Hunted them down like goats or stags, a rifle in hand, a railgun holstered on his back. He fired shots, hitting bodies, bullets blowing through chest cavities, bursting out muscle and bone. He took throat shots, bullets ripping through all those stringy tubes in their necks. He put knives through the children and babes, then decapitated them so he could remove their horns later. He axed the big ones—the berserkers—and took their tusks.

"Should've never come here," he told the laries.

He put larie skulls and bodies in a kiln-like oven and burned their flesh away. He cut through horns with a hacksaw when he didn't have electricity, removing the horns from the skulls. Big laries, small laries, male and female—he didn't discriminate. He placed each horn pair in his collection: a room of shelves in a big Brisbane home.

He killed the half-breeds, too. It didn't matter. He hunted them in jungles, across plains, on the beaches, and rooted them out of their homes and from in between Brisbane's skyscrapers and spires. Nal gave chase across dust-blown hills, hunting those who raced for the borders. He killed, his rage unquenchable. The horns piled high in the jeep's back seats.

You'd see them coming—the jeep fully embossed with horn ornaments and berserker tusks. And the stories of the Horn Man spread to all corners of Australia.

Two years later, he hadn't aged well. His face had creased, tension forming the lines, and his skin was red as a rose, with a black, unkempt beard swathed in dust. People who knew him didn't recognize him.

When the laries had all been run out or killed, along with their human sympathizers, Thaddeus James helped carve the new government in Brisbane. Queensland was alien-free, liberated. Thaddeus anointed Walker and Nal "heroes." They drove the horned jeep through falling confetti and waved to crowds of cheering humans. Thaddeus draped medals around their necks and hosted all the horn hunters and soldiers for a great feast. They raised their glasses to the new nation of Queensland among laughter and cheers.

There being no more laries to hunt, Walker retired, and Nal soon left him. Over the years, the Queensland Guard asked him to train new soldiers and cadets. Schools asked him to speak. He refused.

The world felt like knives to him, he told me, always closing in, and the mere presence of other people wore on him. So he left Brisbane, relocating to a shack out by the old nature reserve north of Beachmere, leaving his horn collection behind. The years vanished, one by one, as he drank alcohol from glass jars, wandered the forests, and hunted yabbies, what we call crayfish, in the streams.

The isolation slowly scraped away at the shell surrounding his sorrow. The power he had once felt from hunting the laries diminished, day by day, as his sorrow nagged him from the inside. He ignored it at first, drinking it away.

That's around the time I met him. About twenty years after the revolution. I did home calls for people living out in the reserves, and I heard about a man who couldn't move. I found him out in the jungle, old and decrepit, a rotten odor hanging around his shack. Next to his bed lay gallon jugs of grog. He wouldn't tell me where he got it from, but he did tell me about his nights.

He awoke in the dark screaming sometimes. Nightmares possessed his sleep, dreams of his dead family in their old house of so long ago. Except his wife, little boys, and daughter...they weren't human; they all had horns. He felt his head, and he, too, had horns. He broke saws and axes and knives on his family's skulls. He burned their flesh off in his kiln, cut them with a diamond blade—no tool could remove the horns. Every night, his family returned no matter what he drank; in the dreams, an army would come to their house, and he'd escape with his family only to be caught by Nal. "Please, let us go. Spare us." He begged her. But she always pulled the trigger on them, saving Walker for last.

When he wasn't dreaming, he'd wake himself up in the middle of the night, talking to no one.

"Forgive me," he'd hear himself say. "Forgive who?" he'd ask me.

But I couldn't tell him. "Men who've done what you've done and seen what you've seen suffer from post-traumatic stress disorder and other psychological issues." Of course, I told him I was no psychologist. "But drinking yourself to death doesn't seem like it's helping." We spoke a while, and he told me about his life and troubles.

After that I didn't call on him for about six months or so. When I finally saw him again, he looked to be in much better health. He could move around again and didn't need his neighbors to bring him his meals anymore. I asked him what changed.

He said one night his son appeared in his dream, horns growing from his head, his mother and the other children stood behind him, all with horns. His small son placed a hand on his knee. "Forgive yourself."

Walker jerked awake, still feeling the hand there as if a ghost had touched him. His gray beard was tear-soaked, and he gut-heaved and shook. Looking into the darkness, he knew that he'd never mourned. He'd disappeared that night his family died, leaving a wake of death between him and his internal pain, and only now had he returned to himself, slowly over the years. The pain from that night now pulsed inside him. The pain forced him to be present, to be in his body. To be who he was: a father, a mourner, a killer, a partner in pain...

He tried to say the words his son had given him, but the heaves worsened, jerking tears from his almost spent ducts.

"I'm sorry," he managed. "I'm sorry. I'm sorry." He lay curled on the floor as the sun peaked over the horizon. He caught a glimpse of himself, an old man, tear-worn, in the stove's reflective metal.

"I forgive you," he whispered.

A DAY IN PARADISE

ELAINE CHAO

56 YEARS AFC

"ARE YOU SURE, Fabiola? It's almost too late." Ives gazed at her, his limpid blue eyes shining against his gaunt face. In some ways, it was a shame that she hadn't chosen him over Claude. Ives had been a steady presence in her life, unlike her soldier husband. The war that had swept up Claude had also toppled the world, casting power against power for the mere promise of inlari technology.

A year ago, Fabiola had kissed her husband farewell for the fourth time in five years, her tummy barely rounded with their second child, and hoped that their land in the Bordeaux hills— land that had been in her family for centuries—would still stand after the War ended. After the birth of baby Isabelle, the newscasts were filled with catastrophe, faraway countries making war against each other for ridiculous reasons. And the French continued their laissez-faire manner of life, making wine and cheese and bread and love, meeting friends and family in cafes across the nation, even while their own loved ones joined the effort to maintain peace in Europe.

During that time, Etienne played amongst the vines, growing strong on well water and sunlight and laughter. Once, when he was nearly three, he found a *vipère* in the log pile, an experience that had frightened him into screaming at the top of his little lungs. Claude came running at the sound and had killed the snake with the axe he used to split wood. Fabiola admitted to herself that Claude had actually been useful that day, unlike the rest of their marriage, where he had talked and sung and danced while she had worked the vines.

Over time, the war, like that snake, crept closer and closer to home. The most worried of her neighbors had already left for neutral countries, and Ives had tried to convince Fabiola, time and time again, to move somewhere else, to New Zealand or South America, somewhere they could continue their lives in relative safety.

He stood in front of her now, the same hopeful question on his face. Poor, foolish Ives, whose heart was always on his sleeve. He had been so helpful after each of her children's births, tending to the vines while she recovered and adjusted to motherhood. Her *maman*, God bless her soul, had patted Ives on the shoulder almost daily, praising him for being the son she never had.

"The war, Ives? Again? Russia and the United States have no bearing on us here." She waved him off, shifting Isabelle to her other hip.

Ives sighed, his thin shoulders bowing forward and making him seem so much older than his thirty years. "I'll be back before I leave," he promised. "I know you want to wait for Claude, but you have to think of the children."

Fabiola watched the rusted red truck rumble off through the rows of healthy vines in the liquid gold of the late afternoon sun. She hadn't wanted to tell Ives, but she'd received notification two weeks ago that Claude had died, his feckless soul trapped in an altercation with the Russians somewhere in the Ural Mountains. But that lie was easy to tell the besotted Ives.

In truth, the only thing she thought about was her children's future. She looked over the acres of land that generations had toiled over and knew that this was her family's legacy. It was Etienne and Isabelle's inheritance, and she planned to teach both of them what it meant to make wine and to be connected to the earth. The rich loam of the valley ran through her veins, something Claude never understood, and even Ives couldn't fathom.

Isabelle whimpered in her arms, her chubby hands patting at Fabiola's chest. The birds still chirped, the insects still whirred in this corner of the world. Fabiola walked back to the house, wondering how long they would last. The only comfort she had in the present crisis was the fact that she lived in the center of a small but powerful nation. Whatever wars were happening out there would take decades, if not longer, to affect their way of life.

Fabiola sat in the swinging chair on the wide porch, keeping an eye on Etienne as he played among the vines. As she swung, Isabelle nursing at her breast, she idly wondered if she should consider selling the land and moving abroad. After all, there were other winemaking regions in the world, places where she could easily leverage her skills to provide for her family. Perhaps it would be better to leave, to flee Europe and go to places where she might thrive. But there were these grapes, this region, this valley. It was almost unconscionable to let the land go.

Etienne's small brown head darted between the vines, his breath coming quickly as he played an incomprehensible game that involved leaping between one row of vines and another. In the midst of a war-torn world, Fabiola breathed in life: the laughter of her child, the insistent pull of her baby on her breast, the grapes ripening on the vine, the sunlight casting deep shadows on the soil. And even though she lived in the darkness of truth, her children still lived in the light, their two little hearts beating in innocence and trusting that the world was as they saw it.

Fabiola brushed the curls away from her daughter's forehead and sent a quick prayer to heaven that her children would never know the ugliness of war. For in the midst of the Bordeaux hills, among streams and a vineyard, this was still paradise.

CHARLIE DINGO

WOELF DIETRICH

98 YEARS AFC

MY UNCLE TOLD me many stories of life after the Great War. When we settled in Australia and the inlaris took over New Zealand, and how, thirty years in, we still lived off the land, toiling the soil and praying to new gods.

One night, when the rain fell hard, and the cracked earth sucked in the moist air, and storm winds threatened to swipe our tin roof from its eaves, we all sat huddled in front of a crackling hearth while my uncle told us the story of Charlie Dingo.

Charlie lived in a dingo hole just outside the small town of Ebor Falls. The townspeople called him crazy for sleeping in the bush with his dogs and other creepy things, right there on the edge of the Amarunta forest, where golden everlasting daisies bloom year round and ground orchids fringe paperbark trees in the summer.

They teased him for preferring the company of canines over human folk and ridiculed him for feeding those scraggy outcasts the rabbit and rat scraps he himself ate.

But the few older folks who remained remembered a different Charlie—a Charlie who had a wife and daughter. A Charlie who managed Ebor Falls' service station and bored patrons most nights in the local pub with booze-fogged tales of his glory days as a sergeant-major in Queensland's militia. Of course, that was back before shrapnel took part of his skull and sent him home with a metal cap and recurring migraines.

They also recalled the events that transformed Charlie from a local town drunk into a mad man who howled at the moon and ran with wild dogs in the surrounding forests. The day an inlari raid party destroyed a farm near the Guy Fawkes river, fifty kilometers from Ebor Falls, where Charlie's wife and daughter had been visiting family, and where Charlie would have been had he not been sleeping one off in the back room of the service station.

When the town's preacher came to deliver news of his family's demise, Murray found Charlie curled up on old crusty blankets, drenched in sweat and dried vomit. The stink of liquor and bile hung so heavy in the room, Murray had to step outside to take a breath.

A bleary-eyed Charlie refused to accept the news at first and staggered back to his home two houses down, calling his wife and daughter's names, but their faded yellow jute was gone. The house was empty except for the neatly made beds and clean kitchen and leftover dinner his wife had set for him at the kitchen table, still covered with a pastry cloth to protect from blow flies.

When Charlie came out the empty house and saw the small group of town's people outside waiting for him, anguish broke over him like a great wave, and he fell to his knees and wailed so loudly, even the dogs on the other side of town cried along.

Ebor Falls' doctor, Abby Tanner, squeezed Charlie's shoulder. Charlie looked up, his red-rimmed eyes pleading. "It's my fault, Abby. I should've been there for them. I just forgot. I promised her I wouldn't drink. I forgot. Oh, dear Lord, I forgot, and now they're dead!"

He buried his face in his hands, and his shoulders shook as he cried. The crowd was stunned into silence as they watched him shrink under the weight of his guilt and sorrow.

Abby tried to say something of comfort, the words barely forming on her lips when Charlie jumped up and plunged through the small crowd. They called after him, but he ignored them and ran. He was in his mid-thirties back then, still powerfully built and stocky, and his legs carried him fast. Maybe he went to search for his wife and daughter's bodies, maybe he went to hunt the inlaris responsible—no one really knew. After a week gone and search parties finding no trace of him, they just assumed he went to live elsewhere or died acting foolish.

Charlie reappeared six months later, a makeshift spear in his hand and four dingoes trailing him. He looked haggard, and the light of madness shone behind his pale blue eyes.

That was many, many years ago.

The town's people's pity lasted only so long. Charlie's presence in Ebor Falls became a bane over time. His heartache, though terrible, was not unique to him alone. Each man, woman, and child there carried scars with them—a gift of burden for being part of the living in a world as equally scarred. They too had suffered at the hands of those alien creatures at one time or another and didn't need some crazy man chasing up ghosts and reminding them what they'd lost. Charlie became a spanner in the works for those who wanted to normalize life and look to the future, and that resentment festered until, many years later, it didn't matter anymore why he became crazy. To them he was a leathery-faced old man, as wild and as useless as the wild dogs he ran with. Charlie Dingo, the town pest. The senile old fool who carried a sorrow so profound, his mind crafted a new reality where even the faint hair on a blade of grass held meaning.

One day when Charlie came into town to fetch water from the pump, some kids were playing on the old tar road that served as Ebor Falls' main street. Pitted with potholes and cracks and crumbling at the sides, and with the infrastructure to keep it maintained nonexistent, it had surrendered to time's harsh demands.

When the kids saw Charlie, they called out to him, cajoling him to howl like a dog. They always did that. Even the adults would fling abuse from time to time, so children needed no invitation to join in.

Charlie ignored them as he usually did and walked on, trailed by four of his scraggly mutts. But nothing much happens in Ebor Falls, and having Charlie come into town was a treat for the brats, a chance to boost excitement and get some laughs. It wasn't long until the chant started. A cruel song of ridicule that some kid had made up many years ago and which had expanded over time and become more elaborate and heartless:

When the night was gray and the moon bright white
and the inlaris came firing their rods of blue-light fright,
to the grave went Charlie's wife and baby daughter
while Charlie dozed from too much lightning water
too late to save his family from the aliens' slaughter
a fool and a coward and a boozer
proclaiming a future filled with blue-light ire

that poor Charlie Dingo, such a liar-liar, pants on fire
as he stalks the woods and curses the moon
waiting for the day he can meet his family soon

Squinting with his sun-bleached eyes and looking straight ahead, Charlie continued to walk on. With his gnarled, leathery hand clasped tightly around the old spear that also served as a walking stick, he mumbled to himself as he ambled past the hardware store with its fake front and faded lettering.

A boy with sandy hair and freckles across his nose would not be ignored, so he hurled a stone that hit one of the dogs on the snout. The dog yelped and charged him, causing the rest of the kids to scamper in a frenzied and very loud panic. Charlie's shrill whistle turned the scraggly beast back, but not before it ripped the boy's trouser leg, drawing blood.

They shot the dog that day and wanted to kill the others, but Charlie begged them not to and promised the mayor and Ebor Falls' only police constable that he would never come to town with the dogs again. He pleaded and made promises and cried and seemed so pathetic that they relented. Charlie disappeared into his forest after that and spoke to no soul again. He took his water from rivers and streams and mostly stayed out of sight.

They caught glimpses of him now and then as he moved among the mallee and shrubs at the forest's edge, setting traps and watching townsfolk go about their daily tasks. Most nights, they could hear his dogs howl as they hunted rabbit and wombat, and sometimes they wondered whether Charlie joined in the howling. The ritual became part of the fabric of life in Ebor Falls.

Until the day it stopped.

The change descended on Ebor Falls as unobtrusively as fog at dawn. That night, the moon cast streaks of crimson silver across the forest floor, and the air felt heavy with the promise of violence. Four berserkers and an inlari officer had come from the Guy Fawkes river, traveling far deeper into the forest than any raiders before them. They slipped through the trees like snakes, slithering between trunks and underbrush, their feet silent on a carpet of needles and leaf litter, hoping to launch a surprise attack on the unsuspecting town, to slaughter and take slaves.

But Charlie Dingo and his strays surprised them, and that night, Charlie and his dogs howled louder than ever before.

The town's people found Charlie's charred body under a gum tree five days later, along with the bodies of his dogs strewn around him in a protective circle. They also discovered the mutilated bodies of a berserker and an inlari officer. Charlie's old spear jutted from the officer's left eye socket. The inlari had made the mistake of leaving his helmet's visor open, and Charlie's spear had found its mark.

They carried his body back to Ebor Falls and buried him in the cemetery there, and every year after that, on the day Charlie Dingo sacrificed himself, the townsfolk honored him and his dogs and declared the day sacred. They would feast at night while the children howled at the moon with arms flailing as they ran through the underbrush, and the adults would talk about Charlie's madness. About his grief and his search for redemption. And each year the sandy-haired boy with freckles across his nose would place a wreath on the spot where Charlie had died.

"The boy that got bitten?" I asked.

My uncle nodded and offered a sad smile. "I felt guilty for throwing that stone. If I hadn't done that, they wouldn't have chased old Charlie away. And yet, because of that incident, Charlie saved our town."

THE RECKONING

DANA LEIPOLD

61 YEARS AFC

THE DOG POUNCED on a mound of dirt, digging with a ferocity that powdered Tarka's feet with earth. Her pale, thin toes disappeared after a moment underneath the deluge.

"Jay, stop! Come!"

The hound paused for a split-second, stared at her, then went back to his task. By now, she'd stepped aside to avoid the mess, but her once white feet turned a brownish color from the moist soil.

"Tarka, it's time. Where are you?"

"But Jay won't stop digging."

Her grandmother, a slim, elderly female, leaned against the doorframe of their dwelling. The setting sun gave her long, spiky horns and ivory hair an orange glow that made her appear as if she were floating.

"Leave the beast. We'll be late."

Tarka tried one last time. "Jay, come!"

The dog continued digging as if his life depended on it. Sighing, Tarka turned to her grandmother, knowing that the animal would most likely be dead in the morning.

"Unfortunately, all beasts act on instinct only."

Her father, mother, and brother gathered their communication devices and blasters, though they would likely not need weapons. Tarka rushed to her chamber, changing from her casual tunic into a sleek black jumpsuit. Brushing back her pale hair, she made sure her horns were shined as much as she could in the span of mere minutes. She smiled brightly at her reflection.

Tonight her family and the *Parhata* soldiers they had trained would officially take control of New Zealand. She imagined her father as *Madeer*, dressed in a traditional yellow robe and his horns polished to sparkle like the stars, leading the first council congregation on Earth with power and grace. His words would inspire inlaris to take their rightful place among these vile *bellogans*—humans. The Great Star Inlar would finally be honored.

Tarka wondered how this species had survived as long as it had. So much violence and infighting, unlike true inlaris. Generations would celebrate her father and this day for millennia. She gathered her own communication device and weapon to join her family at the governing council headquarters and their new home.

Lamps lit the main compound in what would become the new capital of Lakarta, as dusk settled over humans shrieking and sobbing. The Parhata had begun rounding them up at dawn: those that were strong enough were taken to the processing center on hovercrafts; the others were killed. Tarka had heard their cries most of the day, and while she felt a twinge of sympathy, she hoped the whole process would go without incident. If it had been up to her, they would have been at the governing council before dawn, but Father's most trusted advisor recommended that they stay until the last of the *bellogans* in the region were captured. And now it was time.

Following her grandmother into the chaos, Tarka saw them huddled against each other like a frightened herd of animals. A *Parhata* soldier pushed a male *bellogan* toward the others as a female grabbed the soldier, pleading with him. The soldier turned and hit the female over the head with his plasma rifle. A stream of crimson erupted from her left eye. A male attempted to pull the soldier off, but to no avail. The soldier pointed the plasma rifle at the human's head, then led the male back to the group, leaving the female crying and bleeding.

"Quickly now," Tarka's father said. "We don't want to get caught in the reckoning; we've got more important tasks ahead of us."

The last group of *bellogans* was loaded onto the hovercraft as Tarka and her family trotted past, flanked by soldiers. Screams erupted after a soldier fired a blast into the air as the herd scrambled and pushed their way forward. Tarka glanced over her shoulder, their old dwelling now engulfed in flames.

Her brother's idea. A symbol of a new beginning. From the corner of her eye, against the fire's glow, she caught Jay's silhouette running toward kauri trees in the distance.

THE HUNGER KING

M.J. KELLEY

64 YEARS AFC

HE LOST SIGHT of his parents two weeks ago and wasn't sure they survived. A surge of refugees had broken through a barricade outside Brisbane, pushing them through an opening amid gunfire and screams. He'd fallen to the ground and avoided being trampled. Later, as the crowd dispersed, his parents had vanished.

After waiting a few hours, he decided to walk back to Brisbane and return to their family home, maybe knock on doors of friends or classmates from his high school. He wandered the embattled streets, his sojourn disrupted and extended by searches for food and water, and by hiding from soldiers.

Hunger took his voice, took his sense, took his clarity, his reason, so he meandered aimlessly. His hands shook, his stomach clenched, and his thoughts clamored in the murky waters of his brain.

Craters punctured the concrete and pavement, small and large; they dappled the streets, filled with water from the last rain.

Glass, rock, girders, broken beams, drywall, and plastics piled at the building foundations, eroded shale mounds from steep, war-gutted cliffs. He barely recognized the city of his birth and lost himself in the disheveled streets.

At times, hunger focused his attention, piercing his dazed state, directing all his senses for the possibility of food: he saw the tiniest movements; he heard the wind pick up dust and lay it down again; he smelled the metallic residue and paint chips, and the remnants of railgun discharges.

As a rule, he avoided humans and inlaris. He ran from a man and a small girl when they pelted him with stones. He hid from the soldiers. Would he be treated as a larie sympathizer? A refugee? Would he be conscripted, imprisoned? Tortured?

The sun dropped, sending the sky into a pink-purple fury. He scratched the layer of grime on his face, hoping to find an overpass or bridge up ahead. His legs felt wobbly. How long had it been since he ate?

A single alarm boomed on the city's emergency system, then a woman's voice bellowed on the outdoor speakers: "Curfew is sundown. Do not panic. Power will be restored shortly." The occupying army's message blared every hour, unchanging for weeks.

He slid under an overpass and found a mattress of cardboard and garbage already there. He lay his head down and covered his ears. Most nights he took refuge under bridges. The nights were warm, the heat of summer covering him in sweat beads that carved lines on his arms and face, making inlets and crevices in the dirt there. He often woke to the earth-quaking tank treads and marching night patrols; he held still as the bridge struts shuddered.

Railguns woke him, and explosions that cracked open the night. Patrol vehicle spotlights shredded the darkness in quick jerks, men and women speaking in low voices, whispering cautionary tales of blind spots and hidden dangers during night missions. He'd wake to screams, high-pitched horrors, non-human voices, alien executions.

In the mornings, he awoke, surprised he was alive. He felt the twinge of hunger return. And when the pain became unbearable, he strayed from the shade, unsure what to do next, lacking energy to break into apartments and homes and condos and restaurants— most already raided, the food probably gone.

Hobbling along the aqueduct, he saw a male and a female inlari strung up, hanging limp from chains against the concrete wall, cleanly cut stubs where their horns used to be. On a street of office buildings, he saw a dog chase down a cat and eat it.

Later, he traipsed onto a large field and heard children. He watched them from afar as they kicked a deflated ball around. He wanted to ask them for food, but feared retribution. What playground was this? What football field? He pushed around the grass in the overgrown islands between pavement, noticing the concrete's intricate patterns. The pavement formed the strange eminence of an ocean tide, spreading out in concentric circles and swirls, thin tide water frozen in time. All this intricacy to fit the underside of some starship class. That's what this was, the old Brisbane spaceport, one of the first things bombed out in the Great War. Before the war, he remembered carriers and ugets and wedge ships and farlancers and cruisers, giants hanging like clouds in the sky and landing on pads like this one.

When the sun left him again and he gazed upon the muted high-rises, all dark and monolithic against the starry night, he realized he'd zoned out in a daze all day. The children had left—he didn't know when. He thought of his parents, and the mad surge of people at the barricade. He wondered if they'd made it to New South Wales. Did they live?

He fell asleep in the long grass on the landing pad.

The next morning, he eyed puddles speckling a nearby road and considered drinking. He felt the same as he did yesterday, amazed because he thought he'd be dead by now, had even gotten used to the idea.

He hesitated before a deep puddle, recalling how sick another such pool had made him. An orange shape flicked under the surface. All his senses heightened, his fatigue and hunger and dullness seemed to dissipate into the background. A goldfish fluttered about under the water's surface; a broken fish tank, half-submerged, lay next to the puddle.

His arm shot into the water, fingers spread as if they were a net. He startled himself, not realizing at first that the arm belonged to his body. His hand plunged into the water again and again, but the fish was too cunning, too quick. He chased it around the puddle. He shoveled water out, hoping to drain it. When he pulled his hands free, slits of blood formed on his fingers, stinging in the hot air. Invisible glass shards lay in the puddle. He had turned the water murky pink with his blood.

He inhaled deeply, calling on his patience, then he cupped his hands and allowed the goldfish to flit over his palms before flinging his arms upward. One, two, three tries and he scooped the fish up and out of the pool, flinging it away.

Scurrying after it, he caught the fish flopping on the road, gills gasping, drowning in the air. With no hesitation, he picked it up by the tail, leaned his head back and dropped it into his mouth, quickly crushing the fish with his teeth, chewing heartily and swallowing, careful to wipe all the goo from his lips and place it back into his mouth.

With renewed fortitude, he broke into a nearby apartment building and went door to door, kicking them down with vigor. He found crackers, canned soup.

The alarm sounded: "Curfew is sundown. Do not panic. The power will return shortly."

He found a child's paper crown, much like the ones he made with his mother only a few years ago when he was a little kid. He placed the crown on his head, took a cane from by the door, and marched out of the complex like a newly anointed king.

FAR FROM THE ONCE PRISTINE BEACHES AND HIGH RISES AND darkened condos of the coast, far from the landing pad, he wandered, sometimes catching himself singing aloud and then covering his mouth to prevent laughter. He looped his way up to the McRoger Tower, and he realized he'd subconsciously returned to his neighborhood.

He walked up the hill to his old house. The front door was locked, so he jumped the side fence and found the rear sliding glass door smashed in. He stepped through. Broken furniture lay in piles, belongings shredded and strewn about—all the electronics were gone, and when he searched the fridge, a putrid smell burst forth. In the backyard he inspected the half-drained swimming pool.

Plucking a soap bar from the bathroom, he stepped into the placid, warm pool water. He scrubbed himself, the soap stinging in some places. The hourly announcement echoed again but he barely noticed. Soap suds floated among leaves all around him, the walls of the pool encircling him, a canyon of blueish concrete.

When night fell, he searched his room and found his cigarette stash. And in the pantry, in a high cabinet, he found his father's old bottle of American whiskey, the kind no longer made. He packed clothes, first aid, soap, and other supplies into a duffle bag.

Then he climbed out his bedroom window and sat on the roof. He lit a cigarette and took a long drag. Usually he'd feel a pinch of guilt. But not now. His parents were gone; he still hoped they'd lived and were wondering if he was okay. Everything was different. Didn't he deserve a smoke? And a drink?

He looked out over the blackened city and stars strewn in the sky. He'd never seen so many stars while in the city. He'd leave Brisbane, he decided. He had to. More military, more patrols every day. He didn't know what would happen if they found him.

Then one by one, sections of the city blinked on in faded orange glory. Each neighborhood lit up in different square-ish patterns, the street lights waking up and revealing long rows disappearing to the far reaches of the city. Even the high rises flickered on, and the stadium's lights where Thaddeus's army assembled.

Gunfire punched the night air as he smoked. Railguns rattled the quiet. He gazed up. The stars had dimmed, their grandeur dissipated, the night sky diminished in the wake of artificial bulbs. He yawned and stretched, realizing that, for the moment, he was no longer hungry.

THE CARRION HUNTER

WOELF DIETRICH

157 YEARS AFC

A COUPLE OF WEEKS ago, I hit pay dirt. I came across a group of carrions by accident. I'd just buried my pappy, the last of my family members, in the hills of Bandera, and decided to scavenge one of the zero zones for some wreck metal. When my pappy was alive, he never allowed me to visit any of the zero zones. Too dangerous, you see. The sand still glowed there, even a hundred years after the last of the alien and human bombs popped.

I had my old patched-up biohazard suit on. It was just about useless, but I'd grown attached to the thing and wearing it was comfortable and not bad protection against chemical storms. My rucksack was filled with provisions, and I had an ancient FR43 rifle that belonged to my pappy, that he got from his grandpappy, and maybe he got it from his—who knows? Don't much care either. The rifle shoots straight, and the bullets still work.

On my way to one of the zero zones, I crossed into the Valley of Bones, named for a bunch of old bones discovered there many years ago. We thought it used to be a farm or a zoo or something. Anyway, I hadn't been there in years, and it was all just sand now, and when the wind blows, it burned, so I had to be careful. The suits won't last if you stay out in the open too long. But I needed some wreck metal to sell at the floating markets, and, if I was lucky, I might come across a carrion to barter for water. My resources were dwindling.

Anyway, I was scouring the Valley of Bones, and what do you know, down below on the floor littered with yellow and black bones, seven of the carrion fruckers milled around a small hole in an aquifer of glowing red gravel and silt. We have vast underground lakes here, but they are all radioactive, and trust me, you don't want to know about the creatures that live down there. I'm talking beasts as large as what elephants used to be.

Back to my story: hunting a carrion takes a special kind of skill set. See, the thing is, if a carrion touches you, you die. And you don't die quickly. Your flesh rots and melts from your bones like poured liquid steel or melting wax. You'll end up looking like a living skeleton until even your intestines dissolve and your brains leak out your earholes and through the cracks in your exposed skull. But by then you won't have no eyeballs left, anyway. Yeah, you shouldn't fruck with carrions. There's no cure. Hell, there's no cure for Earth. It's rotting away as slowly as a carrion's death touch.

These creatures used to be inlaris, and they mutated over time by whatever weapons the aliens used on us back in the Great War. They have this shiny gelatinous skin with great boils, and sores leaking pus along their shoulders, necks, and stomachs. Long bony fingers end in three-inch black claws, and huge bony spikes erupted through the skin down the ridges of their backs. Which is funny because unlike how inlaris used to look, they don't have any horns on their heads anymore. Just weird thorny stumps.

You should see their mouths. They have rows of razor-sharp, translucent teeth—well, I call them teeth, but they look more like glass shards than normal teeth—and their mouths can open wide enough to rip your face off in one bite. And once you've managed to peel your eyes away from their terrible maws, you'll notice their eyes. Bulbous and shiny red with white pupils. Weird, I know. And frightening.

See, here's the irony and the reason why I hunt carrions. If you capture a carrion and kill it and strip it of flesh and skin, you'll find an iridescent skeletal structure that is worth up to a month's water supply at one of the floating markets. But finding these motherfruckers and catching them has always been a whole different ball game.

The thing is, you can't just kill and skin them. If you do, their bones turn to a black viscous tar that's just as poisonous. For some reason, you have to burn them. They're very flammable, and, once ignited, they burn like a fuse. So I hunt them with bow and flame-tipped arrows, and that alone is a spectacle to behold. I usually aim for the abdomen. It's harder to miss, and once the tip of the arrow pierces their skin, *whoosh!* Just like igniting a match, and as quick. They dance around for a few seconds before plopping down in a smoldering heap. I just tear off the burnt skin and meat afterwards and collect the pretty bones, which are harmless to the touch.

So there I was, basking in my good fortune to have come across a group of carrions like this, and I watched them as they fought over a hole in the ground. They were clawing at each other, even biting. Some frantically tore into the grit and gravel, breaking up thin crusts of stone and splintered bedrock, like they were dying of thirst or something and desperately needed the "magic" water.

I got my gear off and settled by a clump of petrified tree stumps high up on a slope so they couldn't see me. It gave me a good vantage point of the valley floor and the frenzied activity of the creatures down there. Once comfortable, I watched them, and it didn't take long until all of them were sucking dirt water.

Let's be honest, that shit looked hilarious. They were literally kneeling there with their ugly heads pushed deep into the glowing sand, sucking the chemical water below, probably getting mouthfuls of dirt in the process. Frucking idiots.

Right there and then, I decided to bag all of them. They could move pretty fast on their short stubby legs, but if I immobilized them with the FR—and I shot straight and didn't kill them—it'd give me sufficient time to fire off those flame arrows of mine.

A large load of prismatic bones like this lot would be too rich for the floating markets, though. That was a problem. Those merchies—what we called the traders from these floating markets—would slit my throat first rather than allow me such a huge fortune. Naw, with this much purple gold, my best bet would be to travel to Ishuen and sell the bones there.

Ah, Ishuen. It sounded like a grand plan to me. I mean, how could travelling across a harsh, unknown terrain littered with mutated creatures to a mythical domed city that may or may not exist not be a grand thing? My pappy heard stories of Ishuen from his pappy, who heard it from the merchies and other travelers at the floating markets. So my pappy had never been there, of course, and, truth be told, he wasn't even sure it really existed. See, merchies gossip. With so few people around, who knows what is truth or myth these days? Rumors carry the same weight as facts. Facts that over time and distance mutate into stories of mythological proportions. And so we have our own myths and falsehoods that shine with a glint of truth, and to us lost souls here in the wastes, that was enough. Besides, I love a good mystery.

Anyway, so there I was, looking down at seven carrions guzzling "magic" water with their butts in the air and heads in the sand, and I had to act quick while they were still occupied. I unslung my FR. The magazine holds ten rounds, and there were only seven of the fruckers. That would be fine if I shot fast and true. I sat back on my ass, half-leaning against a stump, and pulled the RF to my shoulder, making sure I sighted on the carrion furthest from me. I controlled my breathing, keeping it steady and slow. The only noise came from the growls and fights of the carrions below.

The FR barked against my shoulder, and the first carrion reared up with a shriek that carried past me and echoed up the slopes. The bullet had hit the creature in the ass and passed through its lower back. Before it even hit the ground, I squeezed the trigger again. The FR barked again and again and again, shattering limbs and spines until only the screeching, twisting forms of the mutated inlaris were left on the valley floor, and the FR's loud explosions danced across the slopes.

My pappy was a good teacher. I don't think I ever miss.

After killing those carrions in the valley and burning them, I collected their shiny bones in a large woven bag, along with my gear, and headed back to my podbunker. I had some planning to do. I felt my heart thudding in my chest with excitement as I imagined the bubbled city, glowing like a beacon in the distance.

CHECK OUT
INTERSPECIES!

"Hard-hitting stories about a grim future world...I found the exploration mind-stretching..."—Piers Anthony, *New York Times* bestselling author of the Xanth Series

Fifty years after first contact with the inlaris, war ravaged the Earth, leaving New Zealand and Australia the victors and survivors, but at a devastating cost. As human and inlari factions compete against each other in the struggle for power and resources, some seek zealotry and dominance. Others strive for peace and unity—and with them, hope still lives.

Interspecies is a shared-universe anthology containing four stories of transformation, survival, and the eternal search for meaning and purpose in a turbulent world. Can inlaris and humans alike bridge the gap created by their prejudices? Or will one species forever rule the other?

PICK UP YOUR COPY NOW!

THANK YOU

If you enjoyed this book, we'd love to hear from you.

Consider leaving us a review on your favorite websites:
Amazon
Kobo
Goodreads

We're counting on you.
Thank you for reading and for your support.

AUTHORS

M. J. Kelley is a short fiction aficionado, writer of speculative fiction, and humorist with a passion for education. He's fond of fog and can peel a carrot with a look. M. J. dwells in San Francisco, CA, seasonally as well as year round.

Dana Leipold loves the written word. Her award-winning debut novel, *Burnt Edges*, delves into the dark reaches of abuse and incest while depicting the resilience of one young girl. She practices yoga, loves funny cat videos, and lives in the San Francisco Bay Area with her husband and two children.

Woelf Dietrich mostly writes tales of dark fantasy and the supernatural, which is maybe not such a far cry from his lawyering days. Sometimes he writes other things. He resides in New Zealand with his wife and kids and a dog.

Elaine Chao is obsessed with a number of things, including languages, storytelling, martial arts, music, geeking out, psychology, software, event management, design, and her two cats. At any given point in time, you can find her doing two out of ten in the San Francisco Bay Area.